The Monk and the
Hangman's Daughter

Preface

MANY YEARS AGO – probably in 1890 – Dr Gustav Adolf Danziger brought to me in San Francisco what he said was a translation by himself of a German story by that brilliant writer, Herr Richard Voss, of Heidelberg. As Dr Danziger had at that time a most imperfect acquaintance with the English language, he asked me to rewrite his version of Herr Voss's work for publication in this country. In reading it I was struck by what seemed to me certain possibilities of amplification, and I agreed to do the work if given a free hand by both author and translator. To this somewhat ill-considered proposal, which I supposed would make an end of the matter, I was afterward assured that the author, personally known to the translator, had assented. The result was this book, published by F.J. Schulte & Company of Chicago. Almost coincidently in point of time the publishers failed, and it was, so far as I know, never put upon the market.

Never having seen the original story, and having no skill in German anyhow, I am unable to say what liberties Dr Danziger may have taken with his author's text; to me he professed to have taken none; yet, in recent books of his he is described on the title pages as "Author of The Monk and the Hangman's Daughter" – a statement that seems to justify, if not compel, this brief account of a matter which, though not particularly important, has given rise to more discussion than I have cared to engage in.

By a merely literary artifice the author of the German tale professed to have derived it from another writing, and in the Schulte version appeared the note following:

"The foundation of this narrative is an old manuscript originally belonging to the Franciscan monastery at Berchtesgaden, Bavaria. The manuscript was obtained from a peasant by Herr

Richard Voss, of Heidelberg, from whose German version this is an adaptation."

I have always felt that this was inadequate acknowledgement of the work of Herr Voss, for whom I have the profoundest admiration. Not the least part of my motive and satisfaction in republishing lies in the opportunity that it supplies for doing justice to one to whose splendid imagination the chief credit of the tale is due. My light opinion of the credit due to anyone else is attested by my retention of Dr Danziger's name on the title page. In this version the work that came into my hands from his has been greatly altered and extended.

– Ambrose Bierce

1

O N THE FIRST DAY OF MAY in the year of our Blessed Lord 1680, the Franciscan monks Ægidius, Romanus and Ambrosius were sent by their Superior from the Christian city of Passau to the Monastery of Berchtesgaden, near Salzburg. I, Ambrosius, was the strongest and youngest of the three, being but twenty-one years of age.

The Monastery of Berchtesgaden was, we knew, in a wild and mountainous country, covered with dismal forests, which were infested with bears and evil spirits; and our hearts were filled with sadness to think what might become of us in so dreadful a place. But since it is Christian duty to obey the mandates of the Church, we did not complain, and were even glad to serve the wish of our beloved and revered Superior.

Having received the benediction, and prayed for the last time in the church of our Saint, we tied up our cowls, put new sandals on our feet, and set out, attended by the blessings of all. Although the way was long and perilous, we did not lose our hope, for hope is not only the beginning and the end of religion, but also the strength of youth and the support of age. Therefore our hearts soon forgot the sadness of parting, and rejoiced in the new and varying scenes that gave us our first real knowledge of the beauty of the earth as God has made it. The colour and brilliance of the air were like the garment of the Blessed Virgin; the sun shone like the Golden Heart of the Saviour, from which streameth light and life for all mankind; the dark blue canopy that hung above formed a grand and beautiful house of prayer, in which every blade of grass, every flower and living creature praised the glory of God.

As we passed through the many hamlets, villages and cities that lay along our way, the thousands of people, busy in all the vocations of life, presented to us poor monks a new and strange spectacle, which filled us with wonder and admiration. When so many churches came into view as we journeyed on, and the piety and ardour of the people were made manifest by the acclamations with which they hailed us and their alacrity in ministering to our needs, our hearts were full of gratitude and happiness. All the institutions of the Church were prosperous and wealthy, which showed that they had found favour in the sight of the good God whom we serve. The gardens and orchards of the monasteries, and convents were well kept, proving the care and industry of the pious peasantry and the holy inmates of the cloisters. It was glorious to hear the peals of bells announcing the hours of the day: we actually breathed music in the air – the sweet tones were like the notes of angels singing praise to the Lord.

Wherever we went we greeted the people in the name of our patron Saint. On all sides were manifest humility and joy: women and children hastened to the wayside, crowding about us to kiss our hands and beseech a blessing. It almost seemed as if we were no longer poor servitors of God and man, but lords and masters of this whole beautiful earth. Let us, however, not grow proud in spirit, but remain humble, looking carefully into our hearts lest we deviate from the rules of our holy Order and sin against our blessed Saint.

I, Brother Ambrosius, confess with penitence and shame that my soul caught itself upon exceedingly worldly and sinful thoughts. It seemed to me that the women sought more eagerly to kiss my hands than those of my companions – which surely was not right, since I am not more holy than they; besides, I am younger and less experienced and tried in the fear and commandments of the Lord. When I observed this error of the women, and saw how the maidens kept their eyes upon me, I became frightened, and wondered if I could resist should temptation accost me; and often I thought, with fear and trembling, that vows and prayer and penance alone do not make one a saint; one must be so pure in heart that temptation is unknown. Ah me!

At night we always lodged in some monastery, invariably receiving a pleasant welcome. Plenty of food and drink was set before us, and as we sat at table the monks would crowd about, asking for news of the great world of which it was our blessed privilege to see and learn so much. When our destination was learned we were usually pitied for being doomed to live in the mountain wilderness. We were told of ice fields, snow-crowned mountains and tremendous rock, roaring torrents, caves and gloomy forests; also of a lake so mysterious and terrible that there was none like it in the world. God be with us!

On the fifth day of our journey, while but a short distance beyond the city of Salzburg, we saw a strange and ominous sight. On the horizon, directly in our front, lay a bank of mighty clouds, with many grey points and patches of darker hue, and above, between them and the blue sky, a second firmament of perfect white. This spectacle greatly puzzled and alarmed us. The clouds had no movement; we watched them for hours and could see no change. Later in the afternoon, when the sun was sinking into the west, they became ablaze with light. They glowed and gleamed in a wonderful manner, and looked at times as if they were on fire!

No one can imagine our surprise when we discovered that what we had mistaken for clouds was simply earth and rocks. These, then, were the mountains of which we had heard so much, and the white firmament was nothing else than the snowy summit of the range – which the Lutherans say their faith can remove. I greatly doubt it.

2

WHEN WE STOOD AT THE OPENING of the pass leading into the mountains we were overcome with dejection; it looked like the mouth of Hell. Behind us lay the beautiful country through which we had come, and which now we were compelled to leave for ever; before us frowned the mountains with their inhospitable gorges and haunted forests, forbidding to the sight and full of peril to the body and the soul. Strengthening our hearts with prayer and whispering anathemas against evil spirits, we entered the narrow pass in the name of God; and pressed forwards, prepared to suffer whatever might befall.

As we proceeded cautiously on our way giant trees barred our progress and dense foliage almost shut out the light of day, the darkness being deep and chill. The sound of our footfalls and of our voices, when we dared to speak, was returned to us from the great rocks bordering the pass, with such distinctness and so many repetitions, yet withal so changed, that we could hardly believe we were not accompanied by troops of invisible beings who mocked us and made a sport of our fears. Great birds of prey, startled from their nests in the treetops and the sides of the cliffs, perched upon high pinnacles of rock and eyed us malignly as we passed; vultures and ravens croaked above us in hoarse and savage tones that made our blood run cold. Nor could our prayers and hymns give us peace; they only called forth other fowl and by their own echoes multiplied the dreadful noises that beset us. It surprised us to observe that huge trees had been plucked out of the earth by the roots and hurled down the sides of the hills, and we shuddered to think by what powerful hands this had been done. At times we passed along the edges of high precipices, and the dark chasms that yawned below were a terrible sight. A storm arose, and we were half-blinded by the fires of heaven and stunned by thunder a thousand times louder than we had ever heard. Our fears were at last worked up to so great a degree that we expected every minute to see some devil from Hell leap from behind a rock in our front, or a ferocious bear appear from the undergrowth to dispute our progress. But only deer and foxes crossed our path, and our fears were somewhat quieted to perceive that our blessed Saint was no less powerful in the mountains than on the plains below.

At length we reached the bank of a stream whose silvery waters presented a most refreshing sight. In its crystal depths between the rocks we could see beautiful golden trout as large as the carp in the pond of our monastery at Passau. Even in these wild places Heaven had provided bountifully for the fasting of the faithful.

Beneath the black pines and close to the large lichen-covered rocks bloomed rare flowers of dark blue and golden yellow. Brother Ægidius, who was as learned as pious, knew them from his herbarium and told us their names. We were delighted by the sight of various brilliant beetles and butterflies which had come out of their hiding places after the rain. We gathered handfuls of flowers and chased the pretty winged insects, forgetting our fears and prayers, the bears and evil spirits, in the exuberance of our joy.

For many hours we had not seen a dwelling nor a human being. Deeper and deeper we penetrated the mountain region; greater and greater became the difficulties we experienced in forest and ravine, and all the horrors of the wilderness that we had already passed were repeated, but without so great an effect upon our souls, for we all perceived that the good God was preserving us for longer service to His holy will. A branch of the friendly river lay in our course, and, approaching it, we were delighted to find it spanned by a rough but substantial bridge. As we were about to cross I happened to cast my eyes to the other shore, where I saw a sight that made my blood turn cold with terror. On the opposite bank of the stream was a meadow, covered with beautiful flowers, and in the centre a gallows upon which hung the body of a man!

The face was turned toward us, and I could plainly distinguish the features, which, though black and distorted, showed unmistakable signs that death had come that very day.

I was upon the point of directing my companions' attention to the dreadful spectacle, when a strange incident occurred: in the meadow appeared a young girl, with long golden hair, upon which rested a wreath of blossoms. She wore a bright red dress, which seemed to me to light up the whole scene like a flame of fire. Nothing in her actions indicated fear of the corpse upon the gallows; on the contrary, she glided toward it barefooted through the grass, singing in a loud but sweet voice, and waving her arms to scare away the birds of prey that had gathered about it, uttering harsh cries and with a great buffeting of wings and snapping of beaks. At the girl's approach they all took flight, except one great vulture, which retained its perch upon the gallows and appeared to defy and threaten her. She ran close up to the obscene creature, jumping, dancing, screaming, until it, too, put out its wide wings and flapped heavily away. Then she ceased her dancing, and, taking a position at the gibbet's foot, calmly and thoughtfully looked up at the swinging body of the unfortunate man.

The maiden's singing had attracted the attention of my companions, and we all stood watching the lovely child and her strange surroundings with too much amazement to speak.

While gazing on the surprising scene, I felt a cold shiver run through my body. This is said to be a sure sign that someone has stepped upon the spot which is to be your grave. Strange to say, I felt this chill at the moment the maiden stepped under the gallows. But this only shows how the true beliefs of men are mixed up with foolish superstitions; for how could a sincere follower of Saint Franciscus possibly come to be buried beneath a gallows?

"Let us hasten," I said to my companions, "and pray for the souls of the dead."

We soon found our way to the spot, and, without raising our eyes, said prayers with great fervour; especially did I, for my heart was full of compassion for the poor sinner who hung above.

I recalled the words of God, who said, "Vengeance is mine," and remembered that the dear Saviour had pardoned the thief upon the cross at His side; and who knows that there were not mercy and forgiveness for this poor wretch who had died upon the gallows?

On our approach the maiden had retired a short distance, not knowing what to make of us and our prayers. Suddenly, however, in the midst of our devotions, I heard her sweet, bell-like tones exclaim: "The vulture! the vulture!" and her voice was agitated, as if she felt great fear. I looked up and saw a great grey bird above the pines, swooping downward. It showed no fear of us, our sacred calling and our pious rites. My brothers, however, were indignant at the interruption caused by the child's voice, and scolded her. But I said: "The girl is probably a relation of the dead man. Now think of it, brothers; this terrible bird comes to tear the flesh from his face and feed upon his hands and his body. It is only natural that she should cry out."

One of the brothers said: "Go to her, Ambrosius, and command her to be silent that we may pray in peace for the departed soul of this sinful man."

I walked among the fragrant flowers to where the girl stood with her eyes still fixed upon the vulture, which swung in ever narrowing circles about the gallows. Against a mass of silvery flowers on a bush by which she stood the maid's exquisite figure showed to advantage, as I wickedly permitted myself to observe. Perfectly erect and motionless, she watched my advance, though I marked a terrified look in her large, dark eyes, as if she feared that I would do her harm. Even when I was quite near her she made no movement to come forwards, as women and children usually did, and kiss my hands.

"Who are you?" I said, "and what are you doing in this dreadful place all alone?"

She did not answer me, and made neither sign nor motion; so I repeated my question:

"Tell me, child, what are you doing here?"

"Scaring away the vultures," she replied, in a soft, musical voice, inexpressibly pleasing.

"Are you a relation of the dead man?" I asked.

She shook her head.

"You knew him?" I continued, "and you pity his unchristian death?"

But she was again silent, and I had to renew my questioning: "What was his name, and why was he put to death? What crime did he commit?"

"His name was Nathaniel Alfinger, and he killed a man for a woman," said the maiden, distinctly and in the most unconcerned manner that it is possible to conceive, as if murder and hanging were the commonest and most uninteresting of all events. I was astounded, and gazed at her sharply, but her look was passive and calm, denoting nothing unusual.

"Did you know Nathaniel Alfinger?"

"No."

"Yet you came here to protect his corpse from the fowls?"

"Yes."

"Why do you do that service to one whom you did not know?"

"I always do so."

"How – !"

"Always when anyone is hanged here I come and frighten away the birds and make them find other food. See – there is another vulture!"

She uttered a wild, high scream, threw her arms above her head, and ran across the meadow so that I thought her mad. The big bird flew away, and the maiden came quietly back to me, and, pressing her sunburnt hands upon her breast, sighed deeply, as from fatigue. With as much mildness as I could put into my voice, I asked her:

"What is your name?"

"Benedicta."

"And who are your parents?"

"My mother is dead."

"But your father – where is he?"

She was silent. Then I pressed her to tell me where she lived, for I wanted to take the poor child home and admonish her father to have better care of his daughter and not let her stray into such dreadful places again.

"Where do you live, Benedicta? I pray you tell me."

"Here."

"What! here? Ah, my child, here is only the gallows."

She pointed toward the pines. Following the direction of her finger, I saw among the trees a wretched hut which looked like a habitation more fit for animals than human beings. Then I knew better than she could have told me whose child she was.

When I returned to my companions and they asked me who the girl was, I answered: "The hangman's daughter."

3

HAVING COMMENDED the soul of the dead man to the intercession of the Blessed Virgin and the Holy Saints, we left the accursed spot, but as we withdrew I looked back at the lovely child of the hangman. She stood where I had left her, looking after us. Her fair white brow was still crowned with the wreath of primroses, which gave an added charm to her wonderful beauty of feature and expression, and her large, dark eyes shone like the stars of a winter midnight. My companions, to whom the hangman's daughter was a most unchristian object, reproved me for the interest that I manifested in her; but it made me sad to think this sweet and beautiful child was shunned and despised through no fault of her own. Why should she be made to suffer blame because of her father's dreadful calling? And was it not the purest Christian charity which prompted this innocent maiden to keep the vultures from the body of a fellow creature whom in life she had not even known and who had been adjudged unworthy to live? It seemed to me a more kindly act than that of any professed Christian who bestows money upon the poor. Expressing these feelings to my companions, I found, to my sorrow, that they did not share them; on the contrary, I was called a dreamer and a fool who wished to overthrow the ancient and wholesome customs of the world. Everyone, they said, was bound to execrate the class to which the hangman and his family belonged, for all who associated with such persons would surely be contaminated. I had, however, the temerity to remain steadfast in my conviction, and with due humility questioned the justice of treating such persons as criminals because they were a part of the law's machinery by which criminals were punished. Because in the church the hangman and his family had a dark corner specially set apart for them, that could not absolve us from our duty as servants of the Lord to preach the gospel of justice and mercy and give an example of Christian love and charity. But my brothers grew very angry with me, and the wilderness rang with their loud vociferations, so that I began to feel as if I were very wicked, although unable to perceive my error. I could do nothing but hope that Heaven would be more merciful to us all than we are to one another. In thinking of the maiden it gave me comfort to know that her name was Benedicta. Perhaps her parents had so named her as a means of blessing to one whom no one else would ever bless.

But I must relate what a wonderful country it was into which we were now arrived. Were we not assured that all the world is the Lord's, for He made it, we might be tempted to think such a wild region the kingdom of the Evil One.

Far down below our path the river roared and foamed between great cliffs, the grey points of which seemed to pierce the very sky. On our left, as we gradually rose out of this chasm, was a black forest of pines, frightful to see, and in front of us a most formidable peak. This mountain, despite its terrors, had a comical appearance, for it was white and pointed like a fool's cap, and looked as if some one had put a flour sack on the knave's head. After all, it was nothing but snow. Snow in the middle of the glorious month of May! – surely the works of God are wonderful and almost past belief! The thought came to me that if this old mountain should shake his head the whole region would be full of flying snow.

We were not a little surprised to find that in various places along our road the forest had been cleared away for a space large enough to build a hut and plant a garden. Some of these rude dwellings stood where one would have thought that only eagles would have been bold enough to build; but there is no place, it seems, free from the intrusion of Man, who stretches out his hand for everything, even that which is in the air. When at last we arrived at our destination and beheld the temple and the house erected in this wilderness to the name and glory of our beloved Saint, our hearts were thrilled with pious emotions. Upon the surface of a pine-covered rock was a cluster of huts and houses, the monastery in the midst, like a shepherd surrounded by his flock. The church and monastery were of hewn stone, of noble architecture, spacious and comfortable.

May the good God bless our entrance into this holy place.

4

I HAVE NOW BEEN IN THIS WILDERNESS for a few weeks, but the Lord, too, is here, as everywhere. My health is good, and this house of our beloved Saint is a stronghold of the Faith, a house of peace, an asylum for those who flee from the wrath of the Evil One, a rest for all who bear the burden of sorrow. Of myself, however, I cannot say so much. I am young, and although my mind is at peace, I have so little experience of the world and its ways that I feel myself peculiarly liable to error and accessible to sin. The course of my life is like a rivulet which draws its silver thread smoothly and silently through friendly fields and flowery meadows, yet knows that when the storms come and the rains fall it may become a raging torrent, defiled with earth and whirling away to the sea the wreckage attesting the madness of its passion and its power.

Not sorrow nor despair drew me away from the world into the sacred retreat of the Church, but a sincere desire to serve the Lord. My only wish is to belong to my beloved Saint, to obey the blessed mandates of the Church, and, as a servant of God, to be charitable to all mankind, whom I dearly love. The Church is, in truth, my beloved mother, for, my parents having died in my infancy, I, too, might have perished without care had she not taken pity on me, fed and clothed me and reared me as her own child. And, oh, what happiness there will be for me, poor monk, when I am ordained and receive holy orders as a priest of the Most High God! Always I think and dream of it and try to prepare my soul for that high and sacred gift. I know I can never be worthy of this great happiness, but I do hope to be an honest and sincere priest, serving God and Man according to the light that is given from above. I often pray Heaven to put me to the test of temptation, that I may pass through the fire unscathed and purified in mind and soul. As it is,

I feel the sovereign peace which, in this solitude, lulls my spirit to sleep, and all life's temptations and trials seem far away, like perils of the sea to one who can but faintly hear the distant thunder of the waves upon the beach.

5

OUR SUPERIOR, FATHER ANDREAS, is a mild and pious gentleman. Our brothers live in peace and harmony. They are not idle, neither are they worldly nor arrogant. They are temperate, not indulging too much in the pleasures of the table – a praiseworthy moderation, for all this region, far and wide – the hills and the valleys, the river and forest, with all that they contain – belongs to the monastery. The woods are full of all kinds of game, of which the choicest is brought to our table, and we relish it exceedingly. In our monastery a drink is prepared from malt and barley – a strong, bitter drink, refreshing after fatigue, but not, to my taste, very good.

The most remarkable thing in this part of the country is the salt-mining. I am told that the mountains are full of salt – how wonderful are the works of the Lord! In pursuit of this mineral Man has penetrated deep into the bowels of the earth by means of shafts and tunnels, and brings forth the bitter marrow of the hills into the light of the sun. The salt I have myself seen in red, brown and yellow crystals. The works give employment to our peasants and their sons, with a few foreign labourers, all under the command of an overseer, who is known as the Saltmaster. He is a stern man, exercising great power, but our Superior and the brothers speak little good of him – not from any unchristian spirit, but because his actions are evil, The Saltmaster has an only son. His name is Rochus, a handsome but wild and wicked youth.

6

THE PEOPLE HEREABOUT are a proud, stubborn race. I am told that in an old chronicle they are described as descendants of the Romans, who in their day drove many tunnels into these mountains to get out the precious salt; and some of these tunnels are still in existence. From the window of my cell I can see these giant hills and the black forests which at sunset burn like great firebrands along the crests against the sky.

The forefathers of these people (after the Romans) were, I am told, more stubborn still than they are, and continued in idolatry after all the neighbouring peoples had accepted the cross of the Lord our Saviour. Now, however, they bow their stiff necks to the sacred symbol and soften their hearts to receive the living truth. Powerful as they are in body, in spirit they are humble and obedient to the Word. Nowhere else did the people kiss my hand so fervently as here, although I am not a priest – an evidence of the power and victory of our glorious faith.

Physically they are strong and exceedingly handsome in face and figure, especially the young men; the elder men, too, walk as erect and proud as kings. The women have long golden hair, which they braid and twist about their heads very beautifully, and they love to adorn themselves with jewels. Some have eyes whose dark brilliancy rivals the lustre of the rubies and garnets they wear about their white necks. I am told that the young men fight for the young women as stags for does. Ah, what wicked passions exist in the hearts of men! But since I know nothing of these things, nor shall ever feel such unholy emotions, I must not judge and condemn.

Lord, what a blessing is the peace with which Thou hast filled the spirits of those who are Thine own! Behold, there is no turmoil in my breast; all is calm there as in the soul of a babe which calls "Abba," dear Father. And so may it ever be.

7

I HAVE AGAIN SEEN the hangman's beautiful daughter. As the bells were chiming for mass I saw her in front of the monastery church. I had just come from the bedside of a sick man, and as my thoughts were gloomy the sight of her face was pleasant, and I should have liked to greet her, but her eyes were cast down: she did not notice me. The square in front of the church was filled with people, the men and youths on one side, on the other the women and maidens all clad in their high hats and adorned with their gold chains. They stood close together, but when the poor child approached all stepped aside, whispering and looking askance at her as if she were an accursed leper and they feared infection.

Compassion filled my breast, compelling me to follow the maiden, and, overtaking her, I said aloud: "God greet you, Benedicta."

She shrank away as if frightened, then, looking up, recognised me, seemed astonished, blushed again and again and finally hung her head in silence.

"Do you fear to speak to me?" I asked.

But she made no reply. Again I spoke to her: "Do good, obey the Lord and fear no one: then shall you be saved."

At this she drew a long sigh, and replied in a low voice, hardly more than a whisper: "I thank you, my lord."

"I am not a lord, Benedicta," I said, "but a poor servant of God, who is a gracious and kind Father to all His children, however lowly their estate. Pray to Him when your heart is heavy, and He will be near you."

While I spoke she lifted her head and looked at me like a sad child that is being comforted by its mother. And, still speaking to her out of the great compassion in my heart, I led her into the church before all the people.

But do thou, O holy Franciscus, pardon the sin that I committed during that high sacrament! For while Father Andreas was reciting the solemn words of the mass my eyes constantly wandered to the spot where the poor child knelt in a dark corner set apart for her and her father, forsaken and alone. She seemed to pray with holy zeal, and surely thou didst grace her with a ray of thy favour, for it was through thy love of mankind that thou didst become a great saint, and didst bring before the Throne of Grace thy large heart, bleeding for the sins of all the world. Then shall not I, the humblest of thy followers, have enough of thy spirit to pity this poor outcast who suffers for no sin of her own? Nay, I feel for her a peculiar tenderness, which I cannot help accepting as a sign from Heaven that I am charged with a special mandate to watch over her, to protect her, and finally to save her soul.

8

OUR SUPERIOR HAS SENT FOR ME and rebuked me. He told me I had caused great ill-feeling among the brothers and the people, and asked what devil had me in possession that I should walk into church with the daughter of the public hangman.

What could I say but that I pitied the poor maiden and could not do otherwise than as I did?

"Why did you pity her?" he asked.

"Because all the people shun her," I replied, "as if she were mortal sin itself, and because she is wholly blameless. It certainly is not her fault that her father is a hangman, nor his either, since, alas, hangmen must be."

Ah, beloved Franciscus, how the Superior scolded thy poor servant for these bold words.

"And do you repent?" he demanded at the close of his reproof. But how could I repent of my compassion – incited, as I verily believe, by our beloved Saint?

On learning my obduracy, the Superior became very sad. He gave me a long lecture and put me under hard penance. I took my punishment meekly and in silence, and am now confined in my cell, fasting and chastising myself. Nor in this do I spare myself at all, for it is happiness to suffer for the sake of one so unjustly treated as the poor friendless child.

I stand at the grating of my cell, looking out at the high, mysterious mountains showing black against the evening sky. The weather being mild, I open the window behind the bars to admit the fresh air and better to hear the song of the stream below, which speaks to me with a divine companionship, gentle and consoling.

I know not if I have already mentioned that the monastery is built upon a rock high over the river. Directly under the windows of our cells are the rugged edges of great cliffs, which none can scale but at the peril of his life. Imagine, then, my astonishment when I saw a living figure lift itself up from the awful abyss by the strength of its hands, and, drawing itself across the edge, stand erect upon the very verge! In the dusk I could not make out what kind of creature it was; I thought it some evil spirit come to tempt me; so I crossed myself and said a prayer. Presently there is a movement of its arm, and something flies through the window, past my head, and lies upon the floor of my cell, shining like a white star. I bend and pick it up. It is a bunch of flowers such as I have never seen – leafless, white as snow, soft as velvet, and without fragrance. As I stand by the window, the better to see the wondrous flowers, my eyes turn again to the figure on the cliff, and I hear a sweet, low voice, which says:

"I am Benedicta, and I thank you."

Ah, Heaven! it was the child, who, that she might greet me in my loneliness and penance, had climbed the dreadful rocks, heedless of the danger. She knew, then, of my punishment – knew that it was for her. She knew even the very cell in which I was confined. O holy Saint! surely she could not have known all this but from thee; and I were worse than an infidel to doubt that the feeling which I have for her signifies that a command has been laid upon me to save her.

I saw her bending over the frightful precipice. She turned a moment and waved her hand to me and disappeared. I uttered an involuntary cry – had she fallen? I grasped the iron bars of my window and shook them with all my strength, but they did not yield. In my despair I threw myself upon the floor, crying and praying to all the saints to protect the dear child in her dangerous descent if still she lived, to intercede for her unshriven soul if she had fallen. I was still kneeling when Benedicta gave me a sign of her safe arrival below. It was such a shout as these mountaineers utter in their untamed enjoyment of life – only Benedicta's shout, coming from far below in the gorge, and mingled with its own strange echoes, sounded like nothing I had ever heard from any human throat, and so affected me that I wept, and the tears fell upon the wild flowers in my hand.

9

As a follower of saint franciscus, I am not permitted to own anything dear to my heart, so I have disposed of my most precious treasure; I have presented to my beloved Saint the beautiful flowers which were Benedicta's offering. They are so placed before his picture in the monastery church as to decorate the bleeding heart which he carries upon his breast as a symbol of his suffering for mankind.

I have learned the name of the flower: because of its colour, and because it is finer than other flowers, it is called edelweiss – noble white. It grows in so rare perfection only upon the highest and wildest rocks – mostly upon cliffs, over abysses many hundred feet in depth, where one false step would be fatal to him who gathers it.

These beautiful flowers, then, are the real evil spirits of this wild region; they lure many mortals to a dreadful death. The brothers here have told me that never a year passes but some shepherd, some hunter or some bold youth, attracted by these wonderful blossoms, is lost in the attempt to get them.

May God be merciful to all their souls!

10

I MUST HAVE TURNED PALE when one of the brothers reported at the supper table that upon the picture of Saint Franciscus had been found a bunch of edelweiss of such rare beauty as grows nowhere else in the country but at the summit of a cliff which is more than a thousand feet high, and overhangs a dreadful lake. The brothers tell wondrous tales of the horrors of this lake – how wild its waters and how deep, and how the most hideous spectres are seen along its shores or rising out of it.

Benedicta's edelweiss, therefore, has caused great commotion and wonder, for even among the boldest hunters there are few, indeed, who dare to climb that cliff by the haunted lake. And the tender child has accomplished this feat! She has gone quite alone to that horrible place, and has climbed the almost vertical wall of the mountain to the green spot where the flowers grow with which she was moved to greet me. I doubt not that Heaven guarded her against mishap in order that I might have a visible sign and token that I am charged with the duty of her salvation.

Ah, thou poor sinless child, accurst in the eyes of the people, God hath signified His care of thee, and in my heart I feel already something of that adoration which shall be thy due when for thy purity and holiness He shall bestow upon thy relics some signal mark of His favour, and the Church shall declare thee blessed!

I have learned another thing that I will chronicle here. In this country these flowers are the sign of a faithful love: the youth presents them to his sweetheart, and the maidens decorate the hats of their lovers with them. It is clear that, in expressing her gratitude to a humble servant of the Church, Benedicta was moved, perhaps without knowing it, to signify at the same time her love of the Church itself, although, alas, she has yet too little cause.

As I ramble about here, day after day, I am becoming familiar with every path in the forest, in the dark pass, and on the slopes of the mountains.

I am often sent to the homes of the peasants, the hunters and the shepherds, to carry either medicine to the sick or consolation to the sad. The most reverend Superior has told me that as soon as I receive holy orders I shall have to carry the sacraments to the dying, for I am the youngest and the strongest of the brothers. In these high places it sometimes occurs that a hunter or a shepherd falls from the rocks, and after some days is found, still living. It is then the duty of the priest to perform the offices of our holy religion at the bedside of the sufferer, so that the blessed Saviour may be there to receive the departing soul.

That I may be worthy of such grace, may our beloved Saint keep my heart pure from every earthly passion and desire!

11

T HE MONASTERY HAS CELEBRATED a great festival, and I will report all that occurred.

For many days before the event the brothers were busy preparing for it. Some decorated the church with sprays of pine and birch and with flowers.

They went with the other men and gathered the most beautiful Alpine roses they could find, and as it is midsummer they grow in great abundance. On the day before the festival the brothers sat in the garden, weaving garlands to adorn the church; even the most reverend Superior and the Fathers took pleasure in our merry task. They walked beneath the trees and chatted pleasantly while encouraging the brother butler to spend freely the contents of the cellars.

The next morning was the holy procession. It was very beautiful to see, and added to the glory of our holy Church. The Superior walked under a purple silken canopy, surrounded by the worthy Fathers, and bore in his hands the sacred emblem of the crucifixion of our Saviour. We brothers followed, bearing burning candles and singing psalms. Behind us came a great crowd of the people, dressed in their finest attire.

The proudest of those in the procession were the mountaineers and the salt-miners, the Saltmaster at their head on a beautiful horse adorned with costly trappings. He was a proud-looking man, with his great sword at his side and a plumed hat upon his broad, high brow. Behind him rode Rochus, his son. When we had collected in front of the gate to form a line I took special notice of that young man. I judge him to be self-willed and bold. He wore his hat on the side of his head and cast flaming glances upon the women and the maidens. He looked contemptuously upon us monks. I fear he is not a good Christian, but he is the most beautiful youth that I have ever seen: tall and slender like a young pine, with light brown eyes and golden locks.

The Saltmaster is as powerful in this region as our Superior. He is appointed by the Duke and has judicial powers in all affairs. He has even the power of life and death over those accused of murder or any other abominable crime. But the Lord has fortunately endowed him with good judgment and wisdom.

Through the village the procession moved out into the valley and down to the entrances of the great salt mines. In front of the principal mine an altar was erected, and there our Superior read high mass, while all the people knelt. I observed that the Saltmaster and his son knelt and bent their heads with visible reluctance and this made me very sad. After the service the pro-cession moved toward the hill called "Mount Calvary", which is still higher than the monastery, and from the top of which one has a good view of the whole country below. There the reverend Superior displayed the crucifix in order to banish the evil powers which abound in these terrible mountains; and he also said prayers and pronounced anathemas against all demons infesting the valley below. The bells chimed their praises to the Lord, and it seemed as if divine voices were ringing through the wilderness. It was all, indeed, most beautiful and good.

I looked about me to see if the child of the hangman were present, but I could not see her anywhere, and knew not whether to rejoice that she was out of reach of the insults of the people or to mourn because deprived of the spiritual strength that might have come to me from looking upon her heavenly beauty.

After the services came the feast. Upon a meadow sheltered by trees tables were spread, and the clergy and the people, the most reverend Superior and the great Saltmaster partook of the viands served by the young men. It was interesting to see the young men make big fires of pine and maple, put great pieces of beef upon wooden spits, turn them over the coals until they were brown, and then lay them before the Fathers and the mountaineers. They also boiled mountain trout and carp in large kettles. The wheaten bread was brought in immense baskets, and as to drink, there was assuredly no scarcity of that, for the Superior and the Saltmaster had each given a mighty cask of beer. Both of these monstrous barrels lay on wooden stands under an ancient oak. The boys and the Saltmaster's men drew from the cask which he had given, while that of the Superior was served by the brother butler and a number of us younger monks. In honour of Saint Franciscus I must say that the clerical barrel was of vastly greater size than that of the Saltmaster.

Separate tables had been provided for the Superior and the Fathers, and for the Saltmaster and the best of his people. The Saltmaster and Superior sat upon chairs which stood upon a beautiful carpet, and their seats were screened from the sun by a linen canopy. At the table, surrounded by their beautiful wives and daughters, sat many knights, who had come from their distant castles to share in the great festival. I helped at table. I handed the dishes and filled the goblets and was able to see how good an appetite the company had, and how they loved that brown and bitter drink. I could see also how amorously the Saltmaster's son looked at the ladies, which provoked me very much, as he could not marry them all, especially those already married.

We had music, too. Some boys from the village, who practise on various instruments in their spare moments, were the performers. Ah, how they yelled, those flutes and pipes, and how the fiddle bows danced and chirped! I do not doubt the music was very good, but Heaven has not seen fit to give me the right kind of ears. I am sure our blessed Saint must have derived great satisfaction from the sight of so many people eating and drinking their bellies full. Heavens! how they did eat – what unearthly quantities they did away with! But that was nothing to their drinking. I firmly believe that if every mountaineer had brought along a barrel of his own he would have emptied it, all by himself. But the women seemed to dislike the beer, especially the young girls. Usually before drinking, a young man would hand his cup to one of the maids, who barely touched it with her lips, and, making a grimace, turned away her face. I am not sufficiently acquainted with the ways of woman to say with certainty if this proved that at other times they were so abstemious.

After eating, the young men played at various games which exhibited their agility and strength. Holy Franciscus! what legs they have, what arms and necks! They leapt, they wrestled with one another; it was like the fighting of bears. The mere sight of it caused me to feel great fear. It seemed as if they would crush one another. But the maidens looked on, feeling neither fear nor anxiety; they giggled and appeared well pleased. It was wonderful, too, to hear the voices of these young mountaineers; they threw back their heads and shouted till the echoes rang from the mountain sides and roared in the gorges as if from the throats of a legion of demons.

Foremost among all was the Saltmaster's son. He sprang like a deer, fought like a fiend, and bellowed like a wild bull. Among these mountaineers he was a king. I observed that many were jealous of his strength and beauty, and secretly hated him; yet all obeyed. It was beautiful to see how this young man bent his slender body while leaping and playing in the games – how he threw up his head like a stag at gaze, shook his golden locks and stood in the midst of his fellows with flaming cheeks and sparkling eyes. How sad to think that pride and passion should make their home in so lovely a body, which seems created for the habitation of a soul that would glorify its Maker!

It was near dusk when the Superior, the Saltmaster, the Fathers and all the distinguished guests parted and retired to their homes, leaving the others at drink and dance. My duties compelled me to remain with the brother butler to serve the debauching youths with beer from the great cask. Young Rochus remained too. I do not know how it occurred, but suddenly he stood before me. His looks were dark and his manner proud.

"Are you," he said, "the monk who gave offence to the people the other day?"

I asked humbly – though beneath my monk's robe I felt a sinful anger: "What are you speaking of?"

"As if you did not know!" he said, haughtily. "Now bear in mind what I tell you; if you ever show any friendship toward that girl I shall teach you a lesson which you will not soon forget. You monks are likely to call your impertinence by the name of some virtue; but I know the trick, and will have none of it. Make a note of that, you young cowl-wearer, for your handsome face and big eyes will not save you."

With that he turned his back upon me and went away, but I heard his strong voice ringing out upon the night as he sang and shouted with the others. I was greatly alarmed to learn that this bold boy had cast his eyes upon the hangman's lovely daughter. His feeling for her was surely not honourable, or, instead of hating me for being kind to her, he would have been grateful and would have thanked me. I feared for the child, and again and again did I promise my blessed Saint that I would watch over and protect her, in obedience to the miracle which he has wrought in my breast regarding her. With that wondrous feeling to urge me on, I cannot be slack in my duty, and, Benedicta, thou shalt be saved – thy body and thy soul!

12

L ET ME CONTINUE MY REPORT.

The boys threw dry brushwood into the fire so that the flames illuminated the whole meadow and shone red upon the trees. Then they laid hands upon the village maidens and began to turn and swing them round and round. Holy saints! how they stamped and turned and threw their hats in the air, kicked up their heels, and lifted the girls from the ground, as if the sturdy wenches were nothing but feather balls! They shouted and yelled as if all the evil spirits had them in possession, so that I wished a herd of swine might come, that the devils might leave these human brutes and go into the four-legged ones. The boys were quite full of the brown beer, which for its bitterness and strength is a beastly drink.

Before long the madness of intoxication broke out; they attacked one another with fists and knives, and it looked as if they would do murder. Suddenly the Salt-master's son, who had stood looking on, leapt among them, caught two of the combatants by the hair and knocked their heads together with such force that the blood started from their noses, and I thought surely their skulls had been crushed like egg shells; but they must have been very hard-headed, for on being released they seemed little the worse for their punishment. After much shouting and screaming, Rochus succeeded in making peace, which seemed to me, poor worm, quite heroic. The music set in again: the fiddles scraped and the pipes shrieked, while the boys with torn clothes and scratched and bleeding faces, renewed the dance as if nothing had occurred. Truly, this is a people that would gladden the heart of a Bramarbas or a Holofernes!

I had scarcely recovered from the fright which Rochus had given me, when I was made to feel a far greater one. Rochus was dancing with a tall and beautiful girl, who looked the very queen of this young king. They made such mighty leaps and dizzy turns, but at the same time so graceful, that all looked on with astonishment and pleasure. The girl had a sensuous smile on her lips and a bold look in her brown face, which seemed to say: "See! I am the mistress of his heart!" But suddenly he pushed her from him as in disgust, broke from the circle of dancers, and cried to his friends: "I am going to bring my own partner. Who will go with me?"

The tall girl, maddened by the insult, stood looking at him with the face of a demon, her black eyes burning like flames of hell! But her discomfiture amused the drunken youths, and they laughed aloud.

Snatching a firebrand and swinging it about his head till the sparks flew in showers, Rochus cried again: "Who goes with me?" and walked rapidly away into the forest. The others seizing firebrands also, ran after him, and soon their voices could be heard far away, ringing out upon the night, themselves no longer seen. I was still looking in the direction which they had taken, when the tall girl whom Rochus had insulted stepped to my side and hissed something into my ear. I felt her hot breath on my cheek.

"If you care for the hangman's daughter, then hasten and save her from that drunken wretch. No woman resists him!"

God! how the wild words of that woman horrified me! I did not doubt the girl's words, but in my anxiety for the poor child I asked: "How can I save her?"

"Run and warn her, monk," the wench replied, "she will listen to you."

"But they will find her sooner than I."

"They are drunk and will not go fast. Besides, I know a path leading to the hangman's hut by a shorter route."

"Then show me and be quick!" I cried.

She glided away, motioning me to follow. We were soon in the woods, where it was so dark I could hardly see the woman's figure; but she moved as fast and her step was as sure as in the light of day. Above us we could see the torches of the boys, which showed that they had taken the longer path along the mountain-side. I heard their wild shouts, and trembled for the child. We had walked for some time in silence, having left the youths far behind, when the young woman began speaking to herself. At first I did not understand, but soon my ears caught every passionate word:

"He shall not have her! To the devil with the hangman's whelp! Everyone despises her and spits at the sight of her. It is just like him – he does not care for what people think or say. Because they hate he loves. Besides, she has a pretty face. I'll make it pretty for her! I'll mark it with blood! But if she were the daughter of the devil himself he would not rest until he had her. He shall not!"

She lifted her arms and laughed wildly – I shuddered to hear her! I thought of the dark powers that live in the human breast, though I know as little of them, thank God, as a child.

At length we reached the Galgenberg, where stands the hangman's hut, and a few moments' climb brought us near the door.

"There she lives," said the girl, pointing to the hut, through the windows of which shone the yellow light of a tallow candle; "go warn her. The hangman is ill and unable to protect his daughter, even if he dared. You'd better take her away – take her to the Alpfeld on the Göll, where my father has a house. They will not look for her up there."

With that she left me and vanished in the darkness.

13

LOOKING IN AT THE WINDOW of the hut, I saw the hangman sitting in a chair, with his daughter beside him, her hand upon his shoulder. I could hear him cough and groan, and knew that she was trying to soothe him in his pain. A world of love and sorrow was in her face, which was more beautiful than ever.

Nor did I fail to observe how clean and tidy were the room and all in it. The humble dwelling looked, indeed, like a place blessed by the peace of God. Yet these blameless persons are treated as accurst and hated like mortal sin! What greatly pleased me was an image of the Blessed Virgin on the wall opposite the window at which I stood. The frame was decorated with flowers of the field, and the mantle of the Holy Mother festooned with edelweiss.

I knocked at the door, calling out at the same time: "Do not fear; it is I – Brother Ambrosius."

It seemed to me that, on hearing my voice and name, Benedicta showed a sudden joy in her face, but perhaps it was only surprise – may the saints preserve me from the sin of pride. She came to the window and opened it.

"Benedicta," said I, hastily, after returning her greeting, "wild and drunken boys are on their way hither to take you to the dance. Rochus is with them, and says that he will fetch you to dance with him. I have come before them to assist you to escape."

At the name of Rochus I saw the blood rise into her cheeks and suffuse her whole face with crimson. Alas, I perceived that my jealous guide was right: no woman could resist that beautiful boy, not even this pious and virtuous child. When her father comprehended what I said he rose to his feet and stretched out his feeble arms as if to shield her from harm, but, although his soul was strong, his body, I knew, was powerless. I said to him: "Let me take her away; the boys are drunk and know not what they do. Your resistance would only make them angry, and they might harm you both. Ah, look! See their torches; hear their boisterous voices! Hasten, Benedicta – be quick, be quick!"

Benedicta sprang to the side of the now sobbing old man and tenderly embraced him. Then she hurried from the room, and after covering my hands with kisses ran away into the woods, disappearing in the night, at which I was greatly surprised. I waited for her to return, for a few minutes, then entered the cabin to protect her father from the wild youths who, I thought, would visit their disappointment upon him.

But they did not come. I waited and listened in vain. All at once I heard shouts of joy and screams that made me tremble and pray to the blessed Saint. But the sounds died away in the distance, and I knew that the boys had retraced their steps down the Galgenberg to the meadow of the fires. The sick man and I spoke of the miracle which had changed their hearts, and we were filled with gratitude and joy. Then I returned along the path by which I had come. As I arrived near the meadow, I could hear a wilder and madder uproar than ever, and could see through the trees the glare of greater fires, with the figures of the youths and a few maids dancing in the open, their heads uncovered, their hair streaming over their shoulders, their garments disordered by the fury of their movements. They circled about the fires, wound in and out among them, showing black or red according to how the light struck them, and looking altogether like demons of the pit commemorating some infernal anniversary or some new torment for the damned. And, holy Saviour! there, in the midst of an illuminated space, upon which the others did not trespass, dancing by themselves and apparently forgetful of all else, were Rochus and Benedicta!

14

HOLY MOTHER OF GOD! what can be worse than the fall of an angel? I saw – I understood, then, that in leaving me and her father, Benedicta had gone willingly to meet the very fate from which I had striven to save her!

"The accurst wench has run into Rochus' arms," hissed someone at my side, and, turning, I saw the tall brown girl who had been my guide, her face distorted with hate. "I wish that I had killed her. Why did you suffer her to play us this trick, you fool of a monk?"

I pushed her aside and ran toward the couple without thinking what I did. But what could I do? Even at that instant, as though to prevent my interference, though really unconscious of my presence, the drunken youths formed a circle about them, bawling their admiration and clapping their hands to mark the time.

As these two beautiful figures danced they were a lovely picture. He, tall, slender and lithe, was like a god of the heathen Greeks; while Benedicta looked like a fairy. Seen through the slight mist upon the meadows, her delicate figure, moving swiftly and swaying from side to side, seemed veiled with a web of purple and gold. Her eyes were cast modestly upon the ground; her motions, though agile, were easy and graceful; her face glowed with excitement, and it seemed as if her whole soul were absorbed in the dance. Poor, sweet child! her error made me weep, but I forgave her. Her life was so barren and joyless; why should she not love to dance? Heaven bless her! But Rochus – ah, God forgive him!

While I was looking on at all this, and thinking what it was my duty to do, the jealous girl – she is called Amula – had stood near me, cursing and blaspheming. When the boys applauded Benedicta's dancing Amula made as if she would spring forwards and strangle her. But I held the furious creature back, and, stepping forwards, called out: "Benedicta!"

She started at the sound of my voice, but though she hung her head a little lower, she continued dancing. Amula could control her rage no longer, and rushed forwards with a savage cry, trying to break into the circle. But the drunken boys prevented. They jeered at her, which maddened her the more, and she made effort after effort to reach her victim. The boys drove her away with shouts, curses and laughter. Holy Franciscus, pray for us! – when I saw the hatred in Amula's eyes a cold shudder ran through my body. God be with us! I believe the creature capable of killing the poor child with her own hands, and glorying in the deed!

I ought now to have gone home, but I remained.

I thought of what might occur when the dance was over, for I had been told that the youths commonly accompanied their partners home, and I was horrified to think of Rochus and Benedicta alone together in the forest and the night.

Imagine my surprise when all at once Benedicta lifted her head, stopped dancing, and, looking kindly at Rochus, said in her sweet voice, so like the sound of silver bells:

"I thank you, sir, for having chosen me for your partner in the dance in such a knightly way."

Then, bowing to the Saltmaster's son, she slipped quickly through the circle, and, before anyone could know what was occurring, disappeared in the black spaces of the forest. Rochus at first seemed stupefied with amazement, but when he realised that Benedicta was gone he raved like a madman. He shouted: "Benedicta!" He called her endearing names; but all to no purpose – she had vanished. Then he hurried after her and wanted to search the forest with torches, but the other youths dissuaded him. Observing my presence, he turned his wrath upon me; I think if he had dared he would have struck me. He cried: "I'll make you smart for this, you miserable cowl-wearer!"

But I do not fear him. Praise be to God! Benedicta is not guilty, and I can respect her as before. Yet I tremble to think of the many perils which beset her. She is defenceless against the hate of Amula as well as against the lust of Rochus. Ah, if I could be ever at her side to watch over and protect her! But I commend her to Thee, O Lord: the poor motherless child shall surely not trust to Thee in vain.

15

Alas! my unhappy fate! – again punished and again unable to find myself guilty.

It seems that Amula has talked about Benedicta and Rochus. The brown wench strolled from house to house telling how Rochus went to the gallows for his partner in the dance. And she added that Benedicta had acted in the most shameless manner with the drunken boys. When the people spoke to me of this I enlightened them regarding the facts, as it seemed to me my duty to do, and told all as it had occurred.

By this testimony, in contradiction of one who broke the Decalogue by bearing false witness against her neighbour I have, it seems, offended the Superior. I was summoned before him and accused of defending the hangman's daughter against the statements of an honest Christian girl. I asked, meekly, what I should have done – whether I should have permitted the innocent and defenceless to be calumniated.

"Of what interest," I was asked, "can the hangman's daughter be to you? Moreover, it is a fact that she went of her own will to associate with the drunken boys."

To this I replied: "She went out of love to her father, for if the intoxicated youths had not found her they would have maltreated him – and she loves the old man, who is ill and helpless. Thus it happened, and thus I have testified."

But His Reverence insisted that I was wrong, and put me under severe penance. I willingly undergo it: I am glad to suffer for the sweet child. Nor will I murmur against the revered Superior, for he is my master, against whom to rebel, even in thought, is sin. Is not obedience the foremost commandment of our great saint for all his disciples? Ah, how I long for the priestly ordination and the holy oil! Then I shall have peace and be able to serve Heaven better and with greater acceptance.

I am troubled about Benedicta. If not confined to my cell I should go toward the Galgenberg: perhaps I should meet her. I grieve for her as if she were my sister.

Belonging to the Lord, I have no right to love anything but Him who died upon the cross for our sins – all other love is evil. O blessed Saints in Heaven! what if it be that this feeling which I have accepted as a sign and token that I am charged with the salvation of Benedicta's soul is but an earthly love? Pray for me, O dear Franciscus, that I may have the light, lest I stray into that road which leads down to Hell. Light and strength, beloved Saint, that I may know the right path, and walk therein for ever!

16

I STAND AT THE WINDOW of my cell. The sun sinks and the shadows creep higher on the sides of the mountains beyond the abyss. The abyss itself is filled with a mist whose billowy surface looks like a great lake. I think how Benedicta climbed out of these awful depths to fling me the edelweiss; I listen for the sound of the stones displaced by her daring little feet and plunging into the chasm below. But night after night has passed. I hear the wind among the pines; I hear the water roaring in the deeps; I hear the distant song of the nightingale; but her voice I do not hear.

Every evening the mist rises from the abyss. It forms billows; then rings; then flakes, and these rise and grow and darken until they are great clouds. They cover the hill and the valley, the tall pines and the snow-pointed mountains. They extinguish the last remaining touches of sunlight on the higher peaks, and it is night. Alas, in my soul also there is night – dark, starless and without hope of dawn!

Today is Sunday. Benedicta was not in church – "the dark corner" remained vacant. I was unable to keep my mind upon the service, a sin for which I shall do voluntary penance.

Amula was among the other maidens, but I saw nothing of Rochus. It seemed to me that her watchful black eyes were a sufficient guard against any rival, and that in her jealousy Benedicta would find protection. God can make the basest passions serve the most worthy ends, and the reflection gave me pleasure, which, alas, was of short life.

The services being at an end, the Fathers and friars left the church slowly in procession, moving through the vestry, while the people went out at the main entrance. From the long covered gallery leading out of the vestry one has a full view of the public square of the village. As we friars, who were behind the Fathers, were in the gallery, something occurred which I shall remember even to the day of my death as an unjust deed which Heaven permitted for I know not what purpose. It seems that the Fathers must have known what was coming, for they halted in the gallery, giving us all an opportunity to look out upon the square.

I heard a confused noise of voices. It came nearer, and the shouting and yelling sounded like the approach of all the fiends of Hell. Being at the farther end of the gallery I was unable to see what was going on in the square, so I asked a brother at a window near by what it was all about.

"They are taking a woman to the pillory," he answered.

"Who is it?"

"A girl."

"What has she done?"

"You ask a foolish question. Whom are pillories and whipping-posts for but fallen women?"

The howling mob passed farther into the square, so that I had a full view. In the front were boys, leaping, gesticulating and singing vile songs. They seemed mad with joy and made savage by the shame and pain of their fellow creature. Nor did the maids behave much better. "Fie upon the outcast!" they cried. "See what it is to be a sinner! Thank heaven, we are virtuous."

In the rear of these yelling boys, surrounded by this mob of screaming women and girls – O God! how can I write it? How can I express the horror of it? In the midst of it all – she, the lovely, the sweet, the immaculate Benedicta!

O my Saviour! how did I see all this, yet am still living to relate it? I must have come near to death. The gallery, the square, the people seemed whirling round and round; the earth sank beneath my feet, and, although I strained my eyes open to see, yet all was dark. But it must have been for but a short time; I recovered, and, looking down into the square, saw her again.

They had clothed her in a long grey cloak, fastened at the waist with a rope. Her head bore a wreath of straw, and on her breast, suspended by a string about the neck, was a black tablet bearing in chalk the word "Buhle" – harlot.

By the end of the rope about her waist a man led her. I looked at him closely, and – O most holy Son of God, what brutes and beasts Thou didst come to save! – it was Benedicta's father! They had compelled the poor old man to perform one of the duties of his office by leading his own child to the pillory! I learned later that he had implored the Superior on his knees not to lay this dreadful command upon him, but all in vain.

The memory of this scene can never leave me. The hangman did not remove his eyes from his daughter's face, and she frequently nodded at him and smiled. By the grace of God, the maiden smiled!

The mob insulted her, called her vile names and spat upon the ground in front of her feet. Nor was this all. Observing that she took no notice of them, they pelted her with dust and grass. This was more than the poor father could endure, and, with a faint, inarticulate moan, he fell to the ground in a swoon.

Oh, the pitiless wretches! – they wanted to lift him up and make him finish his task, but Benedicta stretched out her arm in supplication, and with an expression of so ineffable tenderness upon her beautiful face that even the brutal mob felt her gentle power and recoiled before her, leaving the unconscious man upon the ground. She knelt and took her father's head in her lap. She whispered in his ear words of love and comfort. She stroked his grey hair and kissed his pale lips until she had coaxed him into consciousness and he had opened his eyes. Benedicta, thrice blessed Benedicta, thou surely art born to be a saint, for thou didst show a divine patience like that with which our Saviour bore His cross and with it all the sins of the world!

She helped her father to rise, and smiled brightly in his face when he made out to stand. She shook the dust from his clothing, and then, still smiling and murmuring words of encouragement, handed him the rope. The boys yelled and sang, the women screamed, and the wretched old man led his innocent child to the place of shame.

17

WHEN I WAS BACK AGAIN in my cell I threw myself upon the stones and cried aloud to God against the injustice and misery that I had witnessed, and against the still greater misery of which I had been spared the sight. I saw in my mind the father binding his child to the post. I saw the brutal populace dance about her with savage delight. I saw the vicious Amula spit in the pure one's face. I prayed long and earnestly that the poor child might be made strong to endure her great affliction.

Then I sat and waited. I waited for the setting of the sun, for at that time the sufferer is commonly released from the whipping post. The minutes seemed hours, the hours eternities. The sun did not move; the day of shame was denied a night.

It was in vain that I tried to understand it all; I was stunned and dazed. Why did Rochus permit Benedicta to be so disgraced? Does he think the deeper her shame the more easily he can win her? I know not, nor do I greatly care to search out his motive. But, God help me! I myself feel her disgrace, most keenly.

And, Lord, Lord, what a light has come into the understanding of Thy servant! It has come to me like a revelation out of Heaven that my feeling for Benedicta is more and less than what I thought it. It is an earthly love – the love of a man for a woman. As first this knowledge broke into my consciousness my breath beat quick and hard; it seemed to me that I should suffocate. Yet such was the hardness of my heart from witnessing so terrible an injustice tolerated by Heaven, that I was unable wholly to repent. In the sudden illumination I was blinded: I could not clearly see my degree of sin. The tumult of my emotions was not altogether disagreeable; I had to confess to myself that I would not willingly forego it even if I knew it wicked. May the Mother of Mercy intercede for me!

Even now I cannot think that in supposing myself to have a divine mandate to save the soul of Benedicta, and prepare her for a life of sanctity, I was wholly in error. This other human desire – comes it not also of God? Is it not concerned for the good of its object? And what can be a greater good than salvation of the soul? – a holy life on earth, and in Heaven eternal happiness and glory to reward it. Surely the spiritual and the carnal love are not so widely different as I have been taught to think them. They are, perhaps, not antagonistic, and are but expressions of the same will. O holy Franciscus, in this great light that has fallen about me, guide thou my steps. Show to my dazzled eyes the straight, right way to Benedicta's good!

At length the sun disappeared behind the cloister. The flakes and cloudlets gathered upon the horizon; the haze rose from the abyss and, beyond, the purple shadow climbed higher and higher, the great slope of the mountain, extinguishing at last the gleam of light upon the summit. Thank God, oh, thank God, she is free!

18

I HAVE BEEN VERY ILL, but by the kind attention of the brothers am sufficiently recovered to leave my bed. It must be God's will that I live to serve Him, for certainly I have done nothing to merit His great mercy in restoring me to health. Still, I feel a yearning in my soul for a complete dedication of my poor life to Him and His service. To embrace Him and be bound up in His love are now the only aspirations that I have. As soon as the holy oil is on my brow, these hopes, I am sure, will be fulfilled, and, purged of my hopeless earthly passion for Benedicta, I shall be lifted into a new and diviner life. And it may be that then I can, without offence to Heaven or peril to my soul, watch over and protect her far better than I can now as a wretched monk.

I have been weak. My feet, like those of an infant, failed to support my body. The brothers carried me into the garden. With what gratitude I again looked upward into the blue of the sky! How rapturously I gazed upon the white peaks of the mountains and the black forests on their slopes! Every blade of grass seemed to me of special interest, and I greeted each passing insect as if it were an old acquaintance.

My eyes wander to the south, where the Galgenberg is, and I think unceasingly of the poor child of the hangman. What has become of her? Has she survived her terrible experience in the public square? What is she doing? Oh, that I were strong enough to walk to the Galgenberg! But I am not permitted to leave the monastery, and there is none of whom I dare ask her fate. The friars look at me strangely; it is as if they no longer regarded me as one of them. Why is this so? I love them, and desire to live in harmony with them. They are kind and gentle, yet they seem to avoid me as much as they can. What does it all mean?

19

I HAVE BEEN IN THE PRESENCE of the most reverend Superior, Father Andreas. "Your recovery was miraculous," said he. "I wish you to be worthy of such mercies, and to prepare your soul for the great blessing that awaits you. I have, therefore, my son, ordained that you leave us for a season, to dwell apart in the solitude of the mountains, for the double purpose of restoring your strength and affording you an insight into your own heart. Make a severe examination apart from any distractions, and you will perceive, I do not doubt, the gravity of your error. Pray that a divine light may be shed upon your path, that you may walk upright in the service of the Lord as a true priest and apostle, with immunity from all base passions and earthly desires."

I had not the presumption to reply. I submit to the will of His Reverence without a murmur, for obedience is a rule of our Order. Nor do I fear the wilderness, although I have heard that it is infested with wild beasts and evil spirits. Our Superior is right: the time passed in solitude will be to me a season of probation, purification and healing, of which I am doubtless in sore need. So far I have progressed in sin only; for in confession I have kept back many things. Not from the fear of punishment, but because I could not mention the name of the maiden before any other than my holy and blessed Franciscus, who alone can understand. He looks kindly down upon me from the skies, listening to my sorrow; and whatever of guilt there may be in my compassion for the innocent and persecuted child he willingly overlooks for the sake of our blessed Redeemer, who also suffered injustice and was acquainted with grief.

In the mountains it will be my duty to dig certain roots and send them to the monastery. From such roots as I am instructed to gather the Fathers distil a liquor which has become famous throughout the land, even as far, I have been told, as the great city of Munich. This liquor is so strong and so fiery with spices that after drinking it one feels a burning in his throat as if he had swallowed a flame from Hell; yet it is held in high esteem everywhere by reason of its medicinal properties, it being a remedy for many kinds of ills and infirmities; and it is said to be good also for the health of the soul, though I should suppose a godly life might be equally efficacious in places where the liquor cannot be obtained. However this may be, from the sale of the liquor comes the chief revenue of the monastery.

The root from which it is chiefly made is that of an Alpine plant called *gentiana*, which grows in great abundance on the sides of the mountains. In the months of July and August the friars dig the roots and dry them by fire in the mountain cabins, and they are then packed and sent to the monastery. The Fathers have the sole right to dig the root in this region, and the secret of manufacturing the liquor is jealously guarded.

As I am to live in the high country for some time, the Superior has directed me to collect the root from time to time as I have the strength. A boy, a servant in the monastery, is to guide me to my solitary station, carrying up my provisions and returning immediately. He will come once a week to renew my supply of food and take away the roots that I shall have dug.

No time has been lost in dispatching me on my penitential errand. This very evening I have taken leave of the Superior, and, retiring to my cell, have packed my holy books, the *Agnus* and the *Life of St Franciscus*, in a bag. Nor have I forgotten my writing materials with which to continue my diary. These preparations made, I have fortified my soul with prayer, and am ready for any fate, even an encounter with the beasts and demons.

Beloved Saint, forgive the pain I feel in going away without having seen Benedicta, or even knowing what has become of her since that dreadful day. Thou knowest, O glorious one, and humbly do

I confess, that I long to hasten to the Galgenberg, if only to get one glimpse of the hut which holds the fairest and best of her sex. Take me not, holy one, too severely to task, I beseech thee, for the weakness of my erring human heart!

❧ 20

As I left the monastery with my young guide all was quiet within its walls; the holy Brotherhood slept the sleep of peace, which had so long been denied to me. It was early dawn, and the clouds in the east were beginning to show narrow edges of gold and crimson as we ascended the path leading to the mountain. My guide, with bag upon his shoulder, led, and I followed, with my robe fastened back and a stout stick in my hand. This had a sharp iron point which might be used against wild beasts.

My guide was a light-haired, blue-eyed young fellow with a cheerful and amiable face. He evidently found a keen delight in climbing his native hills toward the high country whither we were bound. He seemed not to feel the weight of the burden that he bore; his gait was light and free, his footing sure. He sprang up the steep and rugged way like a mountain goat.

The boy was in high spirits. He told me strange tales of ghosts and goblins, witches and fairies. These last he seemed to be very well acquainted with. He said they appeared in shining garments, with bright hair and beautiful wings, and this description agrees very nearly with what is related of them in books by certain of the Fathers. Anyone to whom they take a fancy, says the boy, they are able to keep under their spell, and no one can break the enchantment, not even the Holy Virgin. But I judge that this is true of only such as are in sin, and that the pure in heart have nothing to fear from them.

We travelled up hill and down, through forests and blooming meadows and across ravines. The mountain streams, hastening down to the valleys, full-banked and noisy, seemed to be relating the wonderful things that they had seen and the strange adventures they had met with on their way. Sometimes the hillsides and the woods resounded with nature's various voices, calling, whispering, sighing, chanting praises to the Lord of all. Now and again we passed a mountaineer's cabin, before which played children, yellow-haired and unkempt. On seeing strangers, they ran away. But the women came forwards, with infants in their arms, and asked for benedictions. They offered us milk, butter, green cheese, and black bread. We frequently found the men seated in front of their huts, carving wood, mostly images of the Saviour upon the cross. These are sent to the city of Munich, where they are offered for sale, bringing, I am told, considerable money and much honour to their pious makers.

At last we arrived at the shore of a lake, but a dense fog prevented a clear view of it. A clumsy little boat was found moored to the bank; my guide bade me enter it, and presently it seemed as if we were gliding through the sky in the midst of the clouds. I had never before been on the water, and felt a terrible misgiving lest we should capsize and drown. We heard nothing but the sound of the ripples against the sides of the boat. Here and there, as we advanced, some dark object became dimly visible for a moment, then vanished as suddenly as it had appeared, and we seemed gliding again through empty space. As the mist at times lifted a little, I observed great black rocks protruding from the water, and not far from shore were lying giant trees half submerged, with huge limbs that looked like the bones of some monstrous skeleton. The scene was so full of horrors that even the joyous youth was silent now, his watchful eye ever seeking to penetrate the fog in search of new dangers.

By all these signs I knew that we were crossing that fearful lake which is haunted by ghosts and demons, and I therefore commended my soul to God. The power of the Lord overcomes all evil. Scarcely had I said my prayer against the spirits of darkness, when suddenly the veil of fog was rent asunder, and like a great rose of fire the sun shone out, clothing the world in garments of colour and gold!

Before this glorious eye of God the darkness fled and was no more. The dense fog, which had changed to a thin, transparent mist, lingered a little on the mountain sides, then vanished quite away. Except in the black clefts of the hills, no vestige of it stayed. The lake was as liquid silver; the mountains were gold, bearing forests that were like flames of fire. My heart was filled with wonder and gratitude.

As our boat crept on I observed that the lake filled a long, narrow basin. On our right the cliffs rose to a great height, their tops covered with pines, but to the left and in front lay a pleasant land, where stood a large building. This was Saint Bartholomæ, the summer residence of his Reverence, Superior Andreas.

This garden spot was of no great extent: it was shut in on all sides but that upon which the lake lay by cliffs that rose a thousand feet into the air. High in the front of this awful wall was set a green meadow, which seemed like a great jewel gleaming upon the grey cloak of the mountain. My guide pointed it out as the only place in all that region where the edelweiss grew. This, then, was the very place where Benedicta had culled the lovely flowers that she had brought to me during my penance. I gazed upward to that beautiful but terrible spot with feelings that I have no words to express. The youth, his mood sympathetic with the now joyous aspect of nature, shouted and sang, but I felt the hot tears rise into my eyes and flow down upon my cheeks, and concealed my face in my cowl.

21

AFTER LEAVING THE BOAT we climbed the mountain. Dear Lord, nothing comes from Thy hand without a purpose and a use, but why Thou shouldst have piled up these mountains, and why Thou shouldst have covered them with so many stones, is a mystery to me, since I can see no purpose in stones, which are a blessing to neither man nor beast.

After hours of climbing we reached a spring, where I sat down, faint and footsore and out of breath. As I looked about me the scene fully justified all that I had been told of these high solitudes. Wherever I turned my eyes was nothing but grey, bare rocks streaked with red and yellow and brown. There were dreary wastes of stones where nothing grew – no single plant nor blade of grass – dreadful abysses filled with ice, and glittering snowfields sloping upward till they seemed to touch the sky.

Among the rocks I did, however, find a few flowers. It seemed as if the Creator of this wild and desolate region had Himself found it too horrible, and, reaching down to the valleys, had gathered a handful of flowers and scattered them in the barren places. These flowers, so distinguished by the Divine hand, have bloomed with a celestial beauty that none others know. The boy pointed out the plant whose root I am to dig, as well as several strong and wholesome herbs serviceable to man, among them the golden-flowered arnica.

After an hour we continued our journey, which we pursued until I was hardly able to drag my feet along the path. At last we reached a lonely spot surrounded by great black rocks. In the centre was a miserable hut of stones, with a low opening in one side for an entrance, and this, the youth told me, was to be my habitation. We entered, and my heart sank to think of dwelling in such a place.

There was no furniture of any kind. A wide bench, on which was some dry Alpine grass, was to be my bed. There was a fireplace, with some wood for fuel, and a few simple cooking utensils.

The boy took up a pan and ran away with it, and, throwing myself down in front of the hut, I was soon lost in contemplation of the wildness and terror of the place in which I was to prepare my soul for service of the Lord. The boy soon returned, bearing the pan in both hands, and on seeing me he gave a joyful shout, whose echoes sounded like a hundred voices babbling among the rocks on every side. After even so short a period of solitude I was so happy to see a human face that I came near answering his greeting with unbecoming joy. How, then, could I hope to sustain a week of isolation in that lonely spot?

When the boy placed the pan before me it was full of milk, and he brought forth from his clothing a pat of yellow butter, prettily adorned with Alpine flowers, and a cake of snow-white cheese wrapped in aromatic herbs. The sight delighted me, and I asked him, jokingly:

"Do butter and cheese, then, grow on stones up here, and have you found a spring of milk?"

"You might accomplish such a miracle," he replied, "but I prefer to hasten to the Black Lake and ask this food of the young women who live there."

He then got some flour from a kind of pantry in the hut, and, having kindled a fire on the hearth, proceeded to make a cake.

"Then we are not alone in this wilderness," I said. "Tell me where is that lake on the shore of which these generous people dwell?"

"The Black Lake," he replied, blinking his eyes, which were full of smoke, "is behind that *Kogel* yonder, and the dairy house stands on the edge of the cliff above the water. It is a bad place. The lake reaches clear down to Hell, and you can hear, through the fissures of the rocks, the roaring and hissing of the flames and the groans of the souls. And in no other place in all this world are there so many fierce and evil spirits. Beware of it! You might fall ill there in spite of your sanctity. Milk and butter and cheese can be obtained at the Green Lake lower down; but I will tell the women to send up what you require. They will be glad to oblige you; and if you will preach them a sermon every Sunday, they will fight the very devil for you!"

After our meal, which I thought the sweetest I had ever eaten, the boy stretched himself in the sunshine and straightway fell asleep, snoring so loudly that, tired as I was, I could hardly follow his example.

22

WHEN I AWOKE THE SUN was already behind the mountains, whose tops were fringed with fire. I felt as one in a dream, but was soon recalled to my senses, and made to feel that I was alone in the wilderness by shouts of the young man in the distance. Doubtless he had pitied my condition, for, instead of disturbing me, he had gone away without taking leave, being compelled to reach the dairy on the Green Lake before nightfall. Entering the cabin, I found a fire burning lustily and a quantity of fuel piled beside it. Nor had the thoughtful youth forgotten to prepare my supper of bread and milk. He had also shaken up the grass on my hard bed, and covered it with a woollen cloth, for which I was truly grateful to him.

Refreshed by my long sleep, I remained outside the cabin till late in the evening. I said my prayers in view of the grey rocks beneath the black sky, in which the stars blinked merrily. They seemed much more brilliant up here than when seen from the valley, and it was easy to imagine that, standing on the extreme summit, one might touch them with his hands.

Many hours of that night I passed under the sky and the stars, examining my conscience and questioning my heart. I felt as if in church, kneeling before the altar and feeling the awful presence of the Lord. And at last my soul was filled with a divine peace, and as an innocent child presses its mother's breast, even so I leaned my head upon thine, O Nature, mother of us all!

23

I HAD NOT BEFORE SEEN A DAWN so glorious! The mountains were rose-red, and seemed almost transparent. The atmosphere was of a silvery lucidity, and so fresh and pure that with every breath I seemed to be taking new life. The dew, heavy and white, clung to the scanty grass blades like rain and dripped from the sides of the rocks.

It was while engaged in my morning devotions that I involuntarily became acquainted with my neighbours. All night long the marmots had squealed, greatly to my dismay, and they were now capering to and fro like hares. Overhead the brown hawks sailed in circles with an eye to the birds flitting among the bushes and the wood mice racing along the rocks. Now and again a troop of chamois passed near, on their way to the feeding grounds on the cliffs, and high above all I saw a single eagle rising into the sky, higher and higher, as a soul flies heavenward when purged of sin.

I was still kneeling when the silence was broken by the sound of voices. I looked about, but, although I could distinctly hear the voices and catch snatches of song, I saw no one. The sounds seemed to come from the heart of the mountain and, remembering the malevolent powers that infest the place, I repeated a prayer against the Evil One and awaited the event.

Again the singing was heard, ascending from a deep chasm, and presently I saw rising out of it three female figures. As soon as they saw me they ceased singing and uttered shrill screams. By this sign I knew them to be daughters of the earth, and thought they might be Christians, and so waited for them to approach.

As they drew near I observed that they carried baskets on their heads, and that they were tall, good-looking lasses, light-haired, brown in complexion and black–eyed. Setting their baskets upon the ground, they greeted me humbly and kissed my hands, after which they opened the baskets and displayed the good things they had brought me – milk, cream, cheese, butter and cakes.

Seating themselves upon the ground, they told me they were from the Green Lake, and said they were glad to have a "mountain brother" again, especially so young and handsome a one; and in saying so there were merry twinkles in their dark eyes and smiles on their red lips, which pleased me exceedingly.

I inquired if they were not afraid to live in the wilderness, at which they laughed, showing their white teeth. They said they had a hunter's gun in their cabin to keep off bears, and knew several powerful sentences and anathemas against demons. Nor were they very lonely, they added, for every Saturday the boys from the valley came up to hunt wild beasts, and then all made merry. I learned from them that meadows and cabins were common among the rocks, where herdsmen and herdswomen lived during the whole summer. The finest meadows, they said, belonged to the monastery, and lay but a short distance away.

The pleasant chatting of the maidens greatly delighted me, and the solitude began to be less oppressive. Having received the benediction, they kissed my hand and went away as they had come, laughing, singing and shouting in the joy of youth and health. So much I have already observed: the people in the mountains lead a better and happier life than those in the damp, deep valleys below. Also, they seem purer in heart and mind, and that may be due to their living so much nearer to Heaven, which some of the brothers say approaches more closely to the earth here than at any other place in the world excepting Rome.

24

T HE MAIDENS HAVING GONE, I stowed away the provisions which
they had brought me, and, taking a short pointed spade and a
bag, went in search of the *gentiana* roots. They grew in abundance,
and my back soon began to ache from stooping and digging; but I
continued the labour, for I desired to send a good quantity to the
monastery to attest my zeal and obedience. I had gone a long distance from my cabin without observing the direction which I had
taken, when suddenly I found myself on the brink of an abyss so
deep and terrible that I recoiled with a cry of horror. At the bottom
of this chasm, so far below my feet that I was giddy to look down, a
small circular lake was visible, like the eye of a fiend. On the shore
of it, near a cliff overhanging the water, stood a cabin, from the
stone-weighted roof of which rose a thin column of blue smoke.
About the cabin, in the narrow and sterile pasture, a few cows and
sheep were grazing. What a dreadful place for a human habitation!

I was still gazing down with fear into this gulf when I was again
startled: I heard a voice distinctly call a name! The sound came
from behind me, and the name was uttered with so caressing
sweetness that I hastened to cross myself as a protection from
the wiles of the fairies with their spells and enchantments. Soon
I heard the voice again, and this time it caused my heart to beat
so that I was near suffocation, for it was Benedicta's! Benedicta in
this wilderness, and I alone with her! Surely I now had need of thy
guidance, blessed Franciscus, to keep my feet in the path of the
Divine purpose.

I turned about and saw her. She was now springing from rock
to rock, looking backward and calling the name that was strange
to me. When she saw that I looked at her she stood motionless.
I walked to her, greeting her in the name of the Blessed Virgin,

though, God forgive me! hardly able in the tumult of my emotions to articulate that holy title.

Ah, how changed the poor child was! The lovely face was as pale as marble; the large eyes were sunken and inexpressibly sad. Her beautiful hair alone was unaltered, flowing over her shoulders like threads of gold. We stood looking at each other, silent from surprise; then I again addressed her:

"Is it, then, you, Benedicta, who live in the cabin down there by the Black Lake – near the waters of Avernus? And is your father with you?"

She made no reply, but I observed a quivering about her delicate mouth, as when a child endeavours to refrain from weeping. I repeated my question: "Is your father with you?"

She answered faintly, in a tone that was hardly more than a sigh: "My father is dead."

I felt a sudden pain in my very heart, and was for some moments unable to speak further, quite overcome by compassion. Benedicta had turned away her face to hide her tears, and her fragile frame was shaken by her sobs. I could no longer restrain myself. Stepping up to her, I took her hand in mine, and, trying to crush back into my secret heart every human desire, and address her in words of religious consolation, said:

"My child – dear Benedicta – your father is gone from you, but another Father remains who will protect you every day of your life. And as far as may accord with His holy will I, too, good and beautiful maiden, help you to endure your great affliction. He whom you mourn is not lost; he is gone to the mercy seat, and God will be gracious to him."

But my words seemed only to awaken her sleeping grief. She threw herself upon the ground and gave way to her tears, sobbing so violently that I was filled with alarm. O Mother of Mercy! how can I bear the memory of the anguish I suffered in seeing this beautiful and innocent child overwhelmed with so great a flood of grief? I bent over her, and my own tears fell upon her golden hair. My heart urged me to lift her from the earth, but my hands were powerless to move. At length she composed herself somewhat and spoke, but as if she were talking to herself rather than to me:

"Oh, my father, my poor, heart-broken father! Yes, he is dead – they killed him – he died long ago of grief. My beautiful mother, too, died of grief – of grief and remorse for some great sin, I know not what, which he had forgiven her. He could only be compassionate and merciful. His heart was too tender to let him kill a worm or a beetle, and he was compelled to kill men. His father and his father's father had lived and died in the Galgenberg. They were hangmen all, and the awful inheritance fell to him: there was no escape, for the terrible people held him to the trade. I have heard him say that he was often tempted to kill himself, and but for me I am sure he would have done so. He could not leave me to starve, though he had to see me reviled, and at last – O Holy Virgin! – publicly disgraced for that of which I was not guilty."

As Benedicta made this reference to the great injustice that she had been made to suffer, her white cheeks kindled to crimson with the recollection of the shame which for her father's sake she had, at the time of it, so differently endured.

During the narrative of her grief she had partly risen and had turned her beautiful face more and more toward me as her confidence had grown; but now she veiled it with her hair, and would have turned her back but that I gently prevented her and spoke some words of comfort, though God knows my own heart was near breaking through sympathy with hers. After a few moments she resumed:

"Alas, my poor father! he was unhappy every way. Not even the comfort of seeing his child baptised was granted him. I was a hangman's daughter, and my parents were forbidden to present me for baptism; nor could any priest be found who was willing to bless me in the name of the Holy Trinity. So they gave me the name Benedicta, and blessed me themselves, over and over again.

"I was only an infant when my beautiful mother died. They buried her in unconsecrated ground. She could not go to the Heavenly Father in the mansions above, but was thrust into the flames. While she was dying my father had hastened to the Reverend Superior, imploring him to send a priest with the sacrament. His prayer was denied. No priest came, and my poor father closed her eyes himself, while his own were blind with tears of anguish for her terrible fate.

"And all alone he had to dig her grave. He had no other place than near the gallows, where he had so often buried the hanged and the accurst. With his own hands he had to place her in that unholy ground, nor could any masses be said for her suffering soul.

"I well remember how my dear father took me then to the image of the Holy Virgin and bade me kneel, and, joining my little hands, taught me to pray for my poor mother, who had stood undefended before the terrible Judge of the Dead. This I have done every morning and evening since that day, and now I pray for both; for my father also has died unshriven, and his soul is not with God, but burns in unceasing fire.

"When he was dying I ran to the Superior, just as he had done for my dear mother. I besought him on my knees. I prayed and wept and embraced his feet, and would have kissed his hand but that he snatched it away. He commanded me to go."

As Benedicta proceeded with her narrative she gained courage. She rose to her feet and stood erect, threw back her beautiful head and lifted her eyes to the heavens as if recounting her wrongs to God's high angels and ministers of doom. She stretched forth her bare arms in gestures of so natural force and grace that I was filled with astonishment, and her unstudied words came from her lips with an eloquence of which I had never before had any conception. I dare not think it inspiration, for – God forgive us all! – every word was an unconscious arraignment of Him and His Holy Church; yet surely no mortal with lips untouched by a live coal from the altar ever so spake before! In the presence of this strange and gifted being I so felt my own unworth that I had surely knelt, as before a blessed saint, but that she suddenly concluded, with a pathos that touched me to tears.

"The cruel people killed him," she said, with a sob in the heart of every word. "They laid hands upon me whom he loved. They charged me falsely with a foul crime. They attired me in a garment of dishonour, and put a crown of straw upon my head, and hung about my neck the black tablet of shame. They spat upon me and reviled me, and compelled him to lead me to the pillory, where I was bound and struck with whips and stones. That broke his great, good heart, and so he died, and I am alone."

25

W HEN BENEDICTA HAD FINISHED I remained silent, for in the presence of such a sorrow what could I say? For such wounds as hers religion has no balm. As I thought of the cruel wrongs of this humble and harmless family there came into my heart a feeling of wild rebellion against the world, against the Church, against God! They were brutally unjust, horribly, devilishly unjust! – God, the Church, and the world.

Our very surrounding – the stark and soulless wilderness, perilous with precipices and bleak with everlasting snows – seemed a visible embodiment of the woeful life to which the poor child had been condemned from birth; and truly this was more than fancy, for since her father's death had deprived her of even so humble a home as the hangman's hovel she had been driven to these eternal solitudes by the stress of want. But below us were pleasant villages, fertile fields, green gardens, and homes where peace and plenty abided all the year.

After a time, when Benedicta was somewhat composed, I asked her if she had anyone with her for protection.

"I have none," she replied. But observing my look of pain, she added: "I have always lived in lonely, accurst places; I am accustomed to that. Now that my father is dead, there is no one who cares even to speak to me, nor any whom I care to talk with – except you." After a pause she said: "True, there is one who cares to see me, but he…"

Here she broke off, and I did not press her to explain lest it should embarrass her. Presently she said:

"I knew yesterday that you were here. A boy came for some milk and butter for you. If you were not a holy man the boy would not have come to me for your food. As it is, you cannot be harmed by the evil which attaches to everything I have or do. Are you sure, though, that you made the sign of the cross over the food yesterday?"

"Had I known that it came from you, Benedicta, that precaution would have been omitted," I answered.

She looked at me with beaming eyes, and said:

"Oh, dear sir, dear Brother!"

And both the look and the words gave me the keenest delight – as, in truth, do all this saintly creature's words and ways.

I inquired what had brought her to the cliff top, and who the person was that I had heard her calling.

"It is no person," she answered, smiling; "it is only my goat. She has strayed away, and I was searching for her among the rocks."

Then nodding to me as if about to say farewell, she turned to go, but I detained her, saying that I would assist her to look for the goat.

We soon discovered the animal in a crevice of rock, and so glad was Benedicta to find her humble companion that she knelt by its side, put her arms about its neck and called it by many endearing names. I thought this very charming, and could not help looking upon the group with obvious admiration. Benedicta, observing it, said:

"Her mother fell from a cliff and broke her neck. I took the little one and brought it up on milk, and she is very fond of me. One who lives alone as I do values the love of a faithful animal."

When the maiden was about to leave me I gained courage to speak to her of what had been so long in my mind. I said: "It is true, is it not, Benedicta, that on the night of the festival you went to meet the drunken boys in order to save your father from harm?"

She looked at me in great astonishment. "For what other reason could you suppose I went?"

"I could not think of any other," I replied, in some confusion.

"And now goodbye, Brother," she said, moving away.

"Benedicta," I cried. She paused and turned her head.

"Next Sunday I shall preach to the dairy women at the Green Lake; will you come?"

"Oh, no, dear Brother," she replied hesitating and in low tones.

"You will not come?"

"I should like to come, but my presence would frighten away the dairy women and others whom your goodness would bring there to hear you. Your charity to me would cause you trouble. I pray you, sir, accept thanks, but I cannot come."

"Then I shall come to you."

"Beware, oh pray, beware!"

"I shall come."

26

THE BOY HAD TAUGHT ME how to prepare a cake. I knew all that went to the making of it, and the right proportions, yet when I tried to make it I could not. All that I was able to make was a smoky, greasy pap, more fit for the mouth of Satan than for a pious son of the Church and follower of Saint Franciscus. My failure greatly discouraged me, yet it did not destroy my appetite; so, taking some stale bread, I dipped it in sour milk and was about to make my stomach do penance for its many sins, when Benedicta came with a basketful of good things from her dairy. Ah, the dear child! I fear that it was not with my heart only that I greeted her that blessed morning.

Observing the smoky mass in the pan, she smiled, and quietly throwing it to the birds (which may Heaven guard!) she cleansed the pan at the spring, and, returning arranged the fire. She then prepared the material for a fresh cake. Taking two handfuls of flour, she put it into an earthen bowl, and upon the top of it poured a cup of cream. Adding a pinch of salt, she mixed the whole vigorously with her slender white hands until it became a soft, swelling dough. She next greased the pan with a piece of yellow butter, and, pouring the dough into it, placed it on the fire. When the heat had penetrated the dough, causing it to expand and rise above the sides of the pan, she deftly pierced it here and there that it should not burst, and when it was well browned she took it up and set it before me, all unworthy as I was. I invited her to share the meal with me, but she would not. She insisted, too, that I should cross myself before partaking of anything that she had brought me or prepared, lest some evil come to me because of the ban upon her; but this I would not consent to do. While I ate she culled flowers from among the rocks, and, making a wreath, hung it upon the cross in front of the cabin; after which, when I had finished, she employed herself in cleansing the dishes and arranging everything in order as it should be, so that I imagined myself far more comfortable than before, even in merely looking about me. When there was nothing more to be done, and my conscience would not permit me to invent reasons for detaining her, she went away, and O my Saviour! how dismal and dreary seemed the day when she was gone. Ah, Benedicta, Benedicta, what is this that thou hast done to me? – making that sole service of the Lord to which I am dedicated seem less happy and less holy than a herdsman's humble life here in the wilderness with thee!

27

L IFE UP HERE is less disagreeable than I thought. What seemed to me a dreary solitude seems now less dismal and desolate. This mountain wilderness, which at first filled me with awe, gradually reveals its benign character. It is marvellously beautiful in its grandeur, with a beauty which purifies and elevates the soul. One can read in it, as in a book, the praises of its Creator. Daily, while digging *gentiana* roots, I do not fail to listen to the voice of the wilderness and to compose and chasten my soul more and more.

In these mountains are no feathered songsters. The birds here utter only shrill cries. The flowers, too, are without fragrance, but wondrously beautiful, shining with the fire and gold of stars. I have seen slopes and heights here which doubtless were never trodden by any human foot. They seem to me sacred, the touch of the Creator still visible upon them, as when they came from His hand.

Game is in great abundance. Chamois are sometimes seen in such droves that the very hillsides seem, to move. There are steinbocks, veritable monsters, but as yet, thank Heaven, I have seen no bears. Marmots play about me like kittens, and eagles, the grandest creatures in this high world, nest in the cliffs to be as near the sky as they can get.

When fatigued, I stretch myself on the Alpine grass, which is as fragrant as the most precious spices. I close my eyes and hear the wind whisper through the tall stems, and in my heart is peace. Blessed be the Lord!

28

EVERY MORNING THE DAIRY women come to my cabin, their merry shouts ringing in the air and echoed from the hills. They bring fresh milk, butter and cheese, chat a little while and go away. Each day they relate something new that has occurred in the mountains or been reported from the villages below. They are joyous and happy, and look forward with delight to Sunday, when there will be divine service in the morning and a dance in the evening.

Alas, these happy people are not free of the sin of bearing false witness against their neighbour. They have spoken to me of Benedicta – called her a disgraceful wench, a hangman's daughter and (my heart rebels against its utterance) the mistress of Rochus! The pillory, they said, was made for such as she.

Hearing these maidens talk so bitterly and falsely of one whom they so little knew, it was with difficulty that I mastered my indignation. But in pity of their ignorance I reprimanded them gently and kindly. It was wrong, I said, to condemn a fellow-being unheard. It was unchristian to speak ill of anyone.

They do not understand. It surprises them that I defend a person like Benedicta – one who, as they truly say, has been publicly disgraced and has not a friend in the world.

29

THIS MORNING I VISITED the Black Lake. It is indeed an awful and accursed place, fit for the habitation of the damned. And there lives the poor forsaken child!

Approaching the cabin, I could see a fire burning on the hearth, and over it was suspended a kettle. Benedicta was seated on a low stool, looking into the flames. Her face was illuminated with a crimson glow, and I could observe heavy tear drops on her cheeks.

Not wishing to see her secret sorrow, I hastened to make known my presence, and addressed her as gently as I could. She was startled, but when she saw who it was, smiled and blushed. She rose and came to greet me, and I began speaking to her almost at random, in order that she might recover her composure. I spoke as a brother might speak to his sister, yet earnestly, for my heart was full of compassion.

"O Benedicta," I said, "I know your heart, and it has more love for that wild youth Rochus than for our dear and blessed Saviour. I know how willingly you bore infamy and disgrace, sustained by the thought that he knew you innocent. Far be it from me to condemn you, for what is holier or purer than a maiden's love? I would only warn and save you from the consequence of having given it to one so unworthy."

She listened with her head bowed, and said nothing, but I could hear her sighs. I saw, too, that she trembled. I continued:

"Benedicta, the passion which fills your heart may prove your destruction in this life and hereafter. Young Rochus is not one who will make you his wife in the sight of God and Man. Why did he not stand forth and defend you when you were falsely accused?"

"He was not there," she said, lifting her eyes to mine, "he and his father were at Salzburg. He knew nothing till they told him."

May God forgive me if at this I felt no joy in another's acquittal of the heavy sin with which I had charged him. I stood a moment irresolute, with my head bowed, silent.

"But, Benedicta," I resumed, "will he take for a wife one whose good name has been blackened in the sight of his family and his neighbours? No, he does not seek you with an honourable purpose. O Benedicta, confide in me. Is it not as I say?"

But she remained silent, nor could I draw from her a single word. She would only sigh and tremble; she seemed unable to speak. I saw that she was too weak to resist the temptation to love young Rochus; nay, I saw that her whole heart was bound up in him, and my soul melted with pity and sorrow – pity for her and sorrow for myself, for I felt that my power was unequal to the command that had been laid upon me. My agony was so keen that I could hardly refrain from crying out.

I went from her cabin, but did not return to my own. I wandered about the haunted shore of the Black Lake for hours, without aim or purpose.

Reflecting bitterly upon my failure, and beseeching God for greater grace and strength, it was revealed to me that I was an unworthy disciple of the Lord and a faithless son of the Church. I became more keenly conscious than I ever had been before of the earthly nature of my love for Benedicta, and of its sinfulness. I felt that I had not given my whole heart to God, but was clinging to a temporal and human hope. It was plain to me that unless my love for the sweet child should be changed to a purely spiritual affection, purified from all the dross of passion, I could never receive holy orders, but should remain always a monk and always a sinner. These reflections caused me great torment, and in my despair I cast myself down upon the earth, calling aloud to my Saviour. In this my greatest trial I clung to the Cross. "Save me, O Lord!" I cried. "I am engulfed in a great passion – save me, oh, save me, or I perish for ever!"

All that night I struggled and prayed and fought against the evil spirits in my soul, with their suggestions of recreancy to the dear Church whose child I am.

"The Church," they whispered, "has servants enough. You are not as yet irrevocably bound to celibacy. You can procure a dispensation from your monastic vows and remain here in the mountains, a layman. You can learn the craft of the hunter or the herdsman, and be ever near Benedicta to guard and guide her – perhaps in time to win her love from Rochus and take her for your wife."

To these temptations I opposed my feeble strength and such aid as the blessed Saint gave me in my great trial. The contest was long and agonising, and more than once, there in the darkness and the wilderness, which rang with my cries, I was near surrender; but at the dawning of the day I became more tranquil, and peace once more filled my heart, even as the golden light filled the great gorges of the mountain where but a few moments before were the darkness and the mist. I thought then of the suffering and death of our Saviour, who died for the redemption of the world, and most fervently I prayed that Heaven would grant me the great boon to die likewise, in a humbler way, even though it were for but one suffering being–Benedicta.

May the Lord hear my prayer!

30

T HE NIGHT BEFORE THE SUNDAY on which I was to hold divine
service, great fires were kindled on the cliffs – a signal for the
young men in the valley to come up to the mountain dairies. They
came in great numbers, shouting and screaming, and were greeted
with songs and shrill cries by the dairy maidens, who swung flaming torches that lit up the faces of the great rocks and sent gigantic
shadows across them. It was a beautiful sight. These are indeed a
happy people.

The monastery boy came in with the rest. He will remain over
Sunday, and, returning, will take back the roots that I have dug. He
gave me much news from the monastery. The reverend Superior
is living at Saint Bartholomæ, fishing and hunting. Another thing
– one which gives me great alarm – is that the Salt-master's son,
young Rochus, is in the mountains not far from the Black Lake. It
seems he has a hunting lodge on the upper cliff, and a path leads
from it directly to the lake. The boy told me this, but did not
observe how I trembled when hearing it. Would that an angel with
a flaming sword might guard the path to the lake, and to Benedicta!

The shouting and singing continued during the whole night, and
between this and the agitation in my soul I did not close my eyes.
Early the next morning the boys and girls arrived in crowds from
all directions. The maidens wore silken kerchiefs twisted prettily
about their heads, and had decorated themselves and their escorts
with flowers.

Not being an ordained priest, it was not permitted me either
to read mass or to preach a sermon, but I prayed with them and
spoke to them whatever my aching heart found to say. I spoke to
them of our sinfulness and God's great mercy; of our harshness
to one another and the Saviour's love for us all; of His infinite

compassion. As my words echoed from the abyss below and the heights above I felt as if I were lifted out of this world of suffering and sin and borne away on angel's wings to the radiant spheres beyond the sky! It was a solemn service, and my little congregation was awed into devotion and seemed to feel as if it stood in the Holy of Holies.

The service being concluded, I blessed the people and they quietly went away. They had not been long gone before I heard the lads send forth ringing shouts, but this did not displease me. Why should they not rejoice? Is not cheerfulness the purest praise a human heart can give?

In the afternoon I went down to Benedicta's cabin and found her at the door, making a wreath of edelweiss for the image of the Blessed Virgin, intertwining the snowy flowers with a purple blossom that looked like blood.

Seating myself beside her, I looked on at her beautiful work in silence, but in my soul was a wild tumult of emotion and a voice that cried: "Benedicta, my love, my soul, I love you more than life! I love you above all things on earth and in Heaven!"

31

T HE SUPERIOR SENT FOR ME, and with a strange foreboding I followed his messenger down the difficult way to the lake and embarked in the boat. Occupied with gloomy reflections and presentiments of impending evil, I hardly observed that we had left the shore before the sound of merry voices apprised me of our arrival at St Bartholomæ. On the beautiful meadow surrounding the dwelling of the Superior were a great number of people – priests, friars, mountaineers and hunters. Many were there who had come from afar with large retinues of servants and boys. In the house was a great bustle – a confusion and a hurrying to and fro, as during a fair. The doors stood wide open, and people ran in and out, clamouring noisily. The dogs yelped and howled as loud as they could. On a stand under the oak was a great cask of beer, and many of the people were gathered about it, drinking. Inside the house, too, there seemed to be much drinking, for I saw many men near the windows with mighty cups in their hands. On entering, I encountered throngs of servants carrying dishes of fish and game. I asked one of them when I could see the Superior. He answered that His Reverence would be down immediately after the meal, and I concluded to wait in the hall. The walls were hung with pictures of some large fish which had been caught in the lake. Below each picture the weight of the monster and the date of its capture, together with the name of the person taking it, were inscribed in large letters. I could not help interpreting these records – perhaps uncharitably – as intimations to all good Christians to pray for the souls of those whose names were inscribed.

After more than an hour the Superior descended the stairs. I stepped forwards, saluting him humbly, as became my position. He nodded, eyed me sharply, and directed me to go to his apartment immediately after supper. This I did.

"How about your soul, my son Ambrosius?" he asked me, solemnly. "Has the Lord shown you grace? Have you endured the probation?"

Humbly, with my head bowed, I answered:

"Most reverend Father, God in my solitude has given me knowledge."

"Of what? Of your guilt?"

This I affirmed.

"Praise be to God!" exclaimed the Superior. "I knew, my son, that solitude would speak to your soul with the tongue of an angel. I have good tidings for you. I have written in your behalf to the Bishop of Salzburg. He summons you to his palace. He will consecrate you and give you holy orders in person, and you will remain in his city. Prepare yourself, for in three days you are to leave us."

The Superior looked sharply into my face again, but I did not permit him to see into my heart. I asked for his benediction, bowed and left him. Ah, then, it was for this that I was summoned! I am to go away for ever. I must leave my very life behind me; I must renounce my care and protection of Benedicta. God help her and me!

32

I AM ONCE MORE IN MY MOUNTAIN HOME, but tomorrow I leave it for ever. But why am I sad? Does not a great blessing await me? Have I not ever looked forward to the moment of my consecration with longing, believing it would bring me the supreme happiness of my life? And now that this great joy is almost within my grasp, I am sad beyond measure.

Can I approach the altar of the Lord with a lie on my lips? Can I receive the holy sacrament as an impostor? The holy oil upon my forehead would turn to fire and burn into my brain, and I should be for ever damned.

I might fall upon my knees before the Bishop and say: "Expel me, for I do not seek after the love of Christ, nor after holy and heavenly things, but after the things of this world."

If I so spoke, I should be punished, but I could endure that without a murmur.

If only I were sinless and could rightly become a priest, I could be of great service to the poor child. I should be able to give her infinite blessings and consolations. I could be her confessor and absolve her from sin, and, if I should outlive her – which God forbid! – might by my prayers even redeem her soul from Purgatory. I could read masses for the souls of her poor dead parents, already in torment.

Above all, if I succeeded in preserving her from that one great and destructive sin for which she secretly longs; if I could take her with me and place her under thy protection, O Blessed Virgin, that would be happiness indeed.

But where is the sanctuary that would receive the hangman's daughter? I know it but too well: when I am gone from here, the Evil One, in the winning shape he has assumed, will prevail, and she will be lost in time and in eternity.

I HAVE BEEN AT BENEDICTA'S CABIN.

"Benedicta," I said, "I am going away from here – away from the mountains – away from you."

She grew pale, but said nothing. For a moment I was overcome with emotion; I seemed to choke, and could not continue. Presently I said: "Poor child, what will become of you? I know that your love for Rochus is strong, and love is like a torrent which nothing can stay. There is no safety for you but in clinging to the cross of our Saviour. Promise me that you will do so – do not let me go away in misery, Benedicta."

"Am I, then, so wicked?" she said, without lifting her eyes from the ground. "Can I not be trusted?"

"Ah, but, Benedicta, the enemy is strong, and you have a traitor to unbar the gates. Your own heart, poor child, will at last betray you."

"He will not harm me," she murmured. "You wrong him, sir, indeed you do."

But I knew that I did not, and was all the more concerned to judge that the wolf would use the arts of the fox. Before the sacred purity of this maiden the base passions of the youth had not dared to declare themselves. But none the less I knew that an hour would come when she would have need of all her strength, and it would fail her. I grasped her arm and demanded that she take an oath that she would throw herself into the waters of the Black Lake rather than into the arms of Rochus. But she would not reply. She remained silent, her eyes fixed upon mine with a look of sadness and reproach which filled my mind with the most melancholy thoughts, and, turning away, I left her.

LORD, SAVIOUR OF MY SOUL, whither hast Thou led me? Here am I in the culprit's tower, a condemned murderer, and tomorrow at sunrise I shall be taken to the gallows and hanged! For whoso slays a fellow being, he shall be slain; that is the law of God and man.

On this the last day of my life I have asked that I be permitted to write, and my prayer is granted. In the name of God and in the truth I shall now set down all that occurred.

Leaving Benedicta, I returned to my cabin, and, having packed everything, waited for the boy. But he did not come: I should have to remain in the mountains another night. I grew restless. The cabin seemed too narrow to hold me; the air was too heavy and hot to sustain life. Going outside, I lay upon a rock and looked up at the sky, dark and glittering with stars. But my soul was not in the heavens; it was at the cabin by the Black Lake.

Suddenly I heard a faint, distant cry, like a human voice. I sat upright and listened, but all was still. It may have been, I thought, the note of some night bird. I was about to lie down again, when the cry was repeated, but it seemed to come from another direction. It was the voice of Benedicta! It sounded again, and now it seemed to come from the air – from the sky above my head, and distinctly it called my name; but, O Mother of God, what anguish was in those tones!

I leapt from the rock. "Benedicta, Benedicta!" I cried aloud. There was no reply.

"Benedicta, I am coming to thee, child!"

I sprang away in the darkness, along the path to the Black Lake. I ran and leapt, stumbling and falling over rocks and stumps of trees. My limbs were bruised, my clothing was torn, but I gave no heed; Benedicta was in distress, and I alone could save and guard her. I rushed on until I reached the Black Lake. But at the cabin all was quiet; there was neither light nor sound; everything was as peaceful as a house of God.

After waiting a long time I left. The voice that I had heard calling me could not have been Benedicta's, but must have been that of some evil spirit mocking me in my great sorrow. I meant to return to my cabin, but an invisible hand directed my steps another way; and although it led me to my death, I know it to have been the hand of the Lord.

Walking on, hardly knowing whither, and unable to find the path by which I had descended, I found myself at the foot of a precipice. Here was a narrow path leading steeply upward along the face of the cliff, and I began ascending it. After I had gone up some distance I looked above, and saw outlined against the starry sky a cabin perched upon the very verge. It flashed through my mind that this was the hunting lodge of the Saltmaster's son, and this the path by which he visited Benedicta. Merciful Father! he, Rochus, was certain to come this way; there could be no other. I would wait for him here.

I crouched in the shadow and waited, thinking what to say to him and imploring the Lord for inspiration to change his heart and turn him from his evil purpose.

Before long I heard him approaching from above. I heard the stones displaced by his foot roll down the steep slopes and leap into the lake far below. Then I prayed God that if I should be unable to soften the youth's heart he might miss his footing and fall, too, like the stones; for it would be better that he should meet a sudden and impenitent death, and his soul be lost, than that he should live to destroy the soul of an innocent girl.

Turning at an angle of the rock, he stood directly before me as, rising, I stepped into the faint light of the new moon. He knew me at once, and in a haughty tone asked me what I wanted.

I replied mildly, explaining why I had barred his way, and begging him to go back. He insulted and derided me.

"You miserable cowler," he said, "will you never cease meddling in my affairs? Because the mountain maids are so foolish as to praise your white teeth and your big black eyes, must you fancy yourself a man, and not a monk? You are no more to women than a goat!"

I begged him to desist and to listen to me. I threw myself on my knees and implored him, however he might despise me and my humble though holy station, to respect Benedicta and spare her. But he pushed me from him with his foot upon my breast. No longer master of myself, I sprang erect, and called him an assassin and a villain.

At this he pulled a dagger from his belt, saying: "I will send you to Hell!"

Quick as a flash of lightning my hand was upon his wrist. I wrested the knife from him and flung it behind me, crying: "Not with weapons, but unarmed and equal, we will fight to the death, and the Lord shall decide!"

We sprang upon each other with the fury of wild animals, and were instantly locked together with arms and hands. We struggled upward and downward along the path, with the great wall of rock on one side, and on the other the precipice, the abyss, the waters of the Black Lake! We writhed and strained for the advantage, but the Lord was against me for He permitted my enemy to overcome me and throw me down on the edge of the precipice. I was in the grasp of a strong enemy, whose eyes glowed like coals of fire. His knee was on my breast and my head hung over the edge – my life was in his hands. I thought he would push me over, but he made no attempt to do so. He held me there between life and death for a dreadful time, then said, in a low, hissing voice: "You see, monk, if I but move I can hurl you down the abyss like a stone. But I care not to take your life, for it is no impediment to me. The girl belongs to me, and to me you shall leave her; do you understand?"

With that he rose and left me, going down the path toward the lake. His footfalls had long died away in the silent night before I was able to move hand or foot. Great God! I surely did not deserve such defeat, humiliation and pain. I had but wished to save a soul, yet Heaven permitted me to be conquered by him who would destroy it!

Finally I was able to rise, although in great pain, for I was bruised by my fall, and could still feel the fierce youth's knee upon my breast and his fingers about my throat. I walked with difficulty back along the path, downward toward the lake. Wounded as I was, I would return to Benedicta's cabin and interpose my body between her and harm. But my progress was slow, and I had frequently to rest; yet it was near dawn before I gave up the effort, convinced that I should be too late to do the poor child the small service of yielding up my remnant of life in her defence.

At early dawn I heard Rochus returning, with a merry song upon his lips. I concealed myself behind a rock, though not in fear, and he passed without seeing me.

At this point there was a break in the wall of the cliff, the path crossing a great crevice that clove the mountain as by a sword stroke from the arm of a Titan. The bottom was strewn with loose boulders and overgrown with brambles and shrubs, through which trickled a slender stream of water fed by the melting snows above. Here I remained for three days and two nights. I heard the boy from the monastery calling my name as he traversed the path searching for me, but I made no answer. Not once did I quench my burning thirst at the brook nor appease my hunger with blackberries that grew abundantly on every side. Thus I mortified the sinful flesh, killed rebellious nature and subdued my spirit to the Lord until at last I felt myself delivered from all evil, freed from the bondage of an earthly love and prepared to devote my heart and soul and life to no woman but thee, O Blessed Virgin!

The Lord having wrought this miracle, my soul felt as light and free as if wings were lifting me to the skies. I praised the Lord in a loud voice, shouting and rejoicing till the rocks rang with the sound. I cried: "Hosanna! Hosanna!" I was now prepared to go before the altar and receive the holy oil upon my head. I was no longer myself. Ambrosius, the poor erring monk, was dead; I was an instrument in the right hand of God to execute His holy will. I prayed for the delivery of the soul of the beautiful maiden, and as I prayed, behold! there appeared to me in the splendour and glory of Heaven the Lord Himself, attended by innumerable angels, filling half the sky! A great rapture enthralled my senses; I was dumb with happiness. With a smile of ineffable benignity God spake to me:

"Because that thou hast been faithful to thy trust, and through all the trials that I have sent upon thee hast not faltered, the salvation of the sinless maiden's soul is now indeed given into thy hand."

"Thou, Lord, knowest," I replied, "that I am without the means to do this work, nor know I how it is to be done."

The Lord commanded me to rise and walk on, and, turning my face away from the glorious Presence, which filled the heart of the cloven mountain with light, I obeyed, leaving the scene of my purgation and regaining the path that led up the face of the cliff. I began the ascent, walking on and on in the splendour of the sunset, reflected from crimson clouds.

Suddenly I felt impelled to stop and look down, and there at my feet, shining red in the cloud light, as if stained with blood, lay the sharp knife of Rochus. Now I understood why the Lord had permitted that wicked youth to conquer me, yet had moved him to spare my life. I had been reserved for a more glorious purpose. And so was placed in my hands the means to that sacred end. My God, my God, how mysterious are Thy ways!

35

YOU SHALL LEAVE HER TO ME." So had spoken the wicked youth while holding me between life and death at the precipice. He permitted me to live, not from Christian mercy, but because he despised my life, a trivial thing to him, not worth taking. He was sure of his prey; it did not matter if I were living or dead.

"You shall leave her to me." Oh, arrogant fool!

Do you not know that the Lord holds His hand over the flowers of the field and the young birds in the nest? Leave Benedicta to you? – permit you to destroy her body and her soul? Ah, you shall see how the hand of God shall be spread above her to guard and save. There is yet time – that soul is still spotless and undefiled. Forwards, then, to fulfil the command of the Most High God!

I knelt upon the spot where God had given into my hand the means of her deliverance. My soul was wholly absorbed in the mission entrusted to me. My heart was in ecstasy, and I saw plainly, as in a vision, the triumphant completion of the act which I had still to do.

I arose, and, concealing the knife in my robe, retraced my steps, going downward toward the Black Lake. The new moon looked like a divine wound in the sky, as if some hand had plunged a dagger into Heaven's holy breast.

Benedicta's door was ajar, and I stood outside a long time, gazing upon the beautiful picture presented to my eyes. A bright fire on the hearth lit up the room. Opposite the fire sat Benedicta, combing her long golden hair. Unlike what it was the last time I had stood before her cabin and gazed upon it, her face was full of happiness and had a glory that I had never imagined in it. A sensuous smile played about her lips while she sang in a low, sweet voice the air of a love song of the people. Ah me! she was beautiful;

she looked like a bride of Heaven. But though her voice was as that of an angel, it angered me, and I called out to her:

"What are you doing, Benedicta, so late in the evening? You sing as if you expected your lover, and arrange your hair as for a dance. It is but three days since I, your brother and only friend, left you, in sorrow and despair. And now you are as happy as a bride."

She sprang up and manifested great joy at seeing me again, and hastened to kiss my hands. But she had no sooner glanced into my face than she uttered a scream of terror and recoiled from me as if I had been a fiend from Hell!

But I approached her and asked: "Why do you adorn yourself so late in the night? – why are you so happy? Have the three days been long enough for you to fall? Are you the mistress of Rochus?"

She stood staring at me in horror. She asked: "Where have you been and why do you come? You look so ill! Sit, sir, I pray you, and rest. You are pale and you shake with cold. I will make you a warm drink and you will feel better."

She was silenced by my stern gaze. "I have not come to rest and be nursed by you," I said. "I am here because the Lord commands. Tell me why you sang."

She looked up at me with the innocent expression of a babe, and replied: "Because I had for the moment forgotten that you were going away, and I was happy."

"Happy?"

"Yes – he has been here."

"Who? Rochus?"

She nodded. "He was so good," she said. "He will ask his father to consent to see me, and perhaps take me to his great house and persuade the Reverend Superior to remove the curse from my life. Would not that be fine? But then," she added, with a sudden change of voice and manner, lowering her eyes, "perhaps you would no longer care for me. It is because I am poor and friendless."

"What! he will persuade his father to befriend you? – to take you to his home? – you, the hangman's daughter? He, this reckless youth, at war with God and God's ministers, will move the Church! Oh, lie, lie, lie! O Benedicta – lost, betrayed Benedicta! By your smiles and by your tears I know that you believe the monstrous promises of this infamous villain."

"Yes," she said, inclining her head as if she were making a confession of faith before the altar of the Lord, "I believe him."

"Kneel, then," I cried, "and praise the Lord for sending one of His chosen to save your soul from temporal and eternal perdition!"

At these words she trembled as in great fear.

"What do you wish me to do?" she exclaimed.

"To pray that your sins may be forgiven."

A sudden rapturous impulse seized my soul. "I am a priest," I cried, "anointed and ordained by God Himself, and in the name of the Father, and of the Son, and of the Holy Spirit, I forgive you your only sin, which is your love. I give you absolution without repentance. I free your soul from the taint of sin because you will atone for it with your blood and life."

With these words, I seized her and forced her down upon her knees. But she wanted to live; she cried and wailed. She clung to my knees and entreated and implored in the name of God and the Blessed Virgin. Then she sprang to her feet and attempted to run away. I seized her again, but she broke away from my grasp and ran to the open door, crying: "Rochus! Rochus! help, oh, help!"

Springing after her, I grasped her by the shoulder, turned her half-round and plunged the knife into her breast.

I held her in my arms, pressed her against my heart and felt her warm blood upon my body. She opened her eyes and fixed upon me a look of reproach, as if I had robbed her of a life of happiness. Then her eyes slowly closed, she gave a long, shuddering sigh, her little head turned upon her shoulder, and so she died.

I wrapped the beautiful body in a white sheet, leaving the face uncovered, and laid it upon the floor. But the blood tinged the linen, so I parted her long golden hair, spreading it over the crimson roses upon her breast. As I had made her a bride of Heaven, I took from the image of the Virgin the wreath of edelweiss and placed it on

91

Benedicta's brow; and now I remembered the edelweiss which she had once brought me to comfort me in my penance.

Then I stirred the fire, which cast upon the shrouded figure and the beautiful face a rich red light, as if God's glory had descended there to enfold her. It was caught and tangled in the golden tresses that lay upon her breast, so that they looked a mass of curling flame.

And so I left her.

36

I DESCENDED THE MOUNTAIN by precipitous paths, but the Lord guided my steps so that I neither stumbled nor fell into the abyss. At the dawning of the day I arrived at the monastery, rang the bell and waited until the gate was opened. The brother porter evidently thought me a fiend, for he raised a howl that aroused the whole monastery. I went straight to the room of the Superior, stood before him in my bloodstained garments, and, telling him for what deed the Lord had chosen me, informed him that I was now an ordained priest. At this they seized me, put me into the tower, and, holding court upon me, condemned me to death as if I were a murderer. Oh, the fools, the poor demented fools!

One person has come to me today in my dungeon, who fell upon her knees before me, kissed my hands and adored me as God's chosen instrument – Amula, the brown maiden. She alone has discovered that I have done a great and glorious deed.

I have asked Amula to chase away the vultures from my body, for Benedicta is in Heaven.

I shall soon be with her. Praise be to God! Hosanna! Amen.

[*To this old manuscript are added the following lines in another hand: "On the fifteenth day of October, in the year of our Lord, 1680, in this place, Brother Ambrosius was hanged, and on the following day his body was buried under the gallows, close to that of the girl Benedicta, whom he killed. This Benedicta, though called the hangman's daughter, was (as is now known through declarations of the youth Rochus) the bastard child of the Saltmaster by the hangman's wife. It is also veritably attested by the same youth that the maiden cherished a secret and forbidden love for him who slew her in ignorance of her passion. In all else Brother Ambrosius was a faithful servant of the Lord. Pray for him, pray for him!"*]

www.oneworldclassics.com